HB

SARATOGA

Pinkerton operative Temple Bywater arrives in Saratoga, Wyoming facing a mystery: who murdered Senator Andrew Stone? Was it his successor, Nathan Wedge? Or were lawyers Forrest and Millard Jackson, and Marshal Tom Gaines involved? Bywater, along with his sidekick Clarence Sugg, and Texas Jack Logan, faces gunmen whose allegiances are unknown. The showdown comes in Saratoga. Will he come out on top in a bloody gun fight against an adversary who is not only tough, but also completely unforeseen?

JIM LAWLESS

SARATOGA

Complete and Unabridged

LINFORD
Leicester

First published in Great Britain in 2008 by
Robert Hale Limited
London

First Linford Edition
published 2009
by arrangement with
Robert Hale Limited
London

British Library CIP Data

Lawless, Jim.
  Saratoga
  1. Western stories.
  2. Large type books.
  I. Title.
  823.9'14–dc22

ISBN 978–1–84782–623–7

Published by
F. A. Thorpe (Publishing)
Anstey, Leicestershire

Set by Words & Graphics Ltd.
Anstey, Leicestershire
Printed and bound in Great Britain by
T. J. International Ltd., Padstow, Cornwall

This book is printed on acid-free paper

*For
Nicholas Hurst
Grandson looking for that
special effect*

1

The ride from Denver, Colorado, to Laramie in the new State of Wyoming took Temple Bywater two days, the stiff traverse in a westerly direction across the rugged northern flank of the Medicine Bow Mountains most of the next. On that third night he camped below a hog-back ridge, ate with his back against a tree then enjoyed an after-supper cigarette. Stars twinkled in dark velvet skies. The soft night sounds were all around him as he gazed pensively down at the distant lights of Saratoga on the North Platte river. One more day, he reckoned. Then he would be better able to assess the manner of men he would be pitted against; the dangers he would inevitably face; the complexities of the problem he had been despatched to resolve. As he pondered, in his imagination the scale of what lay ahead became magnified out of all proportion. Disturbing thoughts nagged, like an unwelcome toothache guaranteeing a restless night.

Saratoga was his destination — but would he make it to the small town on the North Platte? Had the men who committed the serious crime that had drawn him to the region, heard of his movements? Were they even now awaiting his arrival, planning a welcoming committee that would put an end to his efforts before they had begun?

Had this mission, from its outset, been doomed to failure?

Only time would bring the answer, Bywater thought, flashing a grim smile at the stars to banish morbid thoughts. He finished his cigarette, ground it beneath his boot heel and rolled into his blankets.

He was awake with the dawn. Under dark, dripping lodgepole pines he washed and shaved at a tumbling creek in a strange, misty half light, shivering at the bite of icy mountain water on his naked skin. Watching the vapour of his own breath on the crisp air, he breakfasted on jerky washed down with more of the clear cold water, looking ahead in his thoughts as he chewed.

Saratoga was the first stage, if he made it. Once there he would meet people in authority, ask questions, listen, and let the citizens of Saratoga become accustomed to his presence. He would embark on the second, dangerous stage some time after noon — and with that second stage he would be entering uncharted territory, because advance planning could go only so far.

He shook his head irritably. Enough! A man could spend only so long thinking before thoughts became muddled and lost their value. It was time for action.

The early morning sun was casting a long shadow as he broke camp, swung into the saddle and pointed Lorna Doone downhill. As was his custom he gave the big black mare her head, allowing her to carry him down the rutted slopes of the western foothills without interference. On the steeper inclines he tilted his gaunt frame backwards in the saddle, swaying to his mount's twists and turns, gripping fiercely with his knees. His gloved hands held the reins with delicacy as the big horse picked its way across dangerous terrain where an error of judgement could mean a snapped leg.

So complete was Bywater's confidence in Doone that he found his thoughts drifting. Once, he slipped into a half doze, only to snap back to full consciousness, grinning at his own stupidity.

Amusement was still lingering when the rifle shot cracked in the still air. The sound was distant, as faint as the snapping of a dry twig and swiftly receding in a series of flat echoes. But to a man engaged in Temple Bywater's hazardous occupation, and with his years of experience, it was unmistakable. Shock brought instant gravity, and with it an acute awareness of deadly danger.

Bywater drew rein. He held the trembling black mare still, whispered softly to it, leaned forward absently to pat the glistening neck. Under his tugged-down hat brim his eyes were busy scanning the lower slopes for the telltale wisp of smoke. Half listening for the drum of hoofs that would mean the bushwhacker was making his escape, he noted that following the shot there had been no hum of hot lead close to his ear, no soft thud as a slug buried itself in the mountainside. Also, he was still alive.

Again the grin. Alive now — but if the first shot truly had been intended for him, what if there was a second? And what the hell was he doing standing still? On the open slopes, he was a sitting duck.

Bywater straightened in the saddle. 'Come on, Doone,' he said softly, and touching the willing mare's flanks with his heels he began pushing hard downhill. After ten minutes' reckless riding the ground began levelling. He was entering a gently undulating area of sagebrush and rough scrub. Dusty cottonwoods lined a dry creek bed. The trail followed its tortuous course.

Bywater eased back, slowed the mare to a walk. His skin crawled in the oppressive silence. The thick scrub afforded a thousand hiding places, and instinct told Bywater that from one of them the gunman was watching him along the blued barrel of a rifle. Frustration warned him that pressing on without knowing the man's location was foolhardy but, short of turning tail and heading back for the dubious safety of the forested high country, there was nothing he could do. If pushing on was foolish, he thought ruefully, retreating was to invite a bullet in the back.

He was still undecided when the hidden gunman squeezed the trigger and loosed his second shot. But this one Bywater didn't hear. He was aware of a mighty blow in the belly. Of the breath being driven from his body. Then he was falling backwards out of the saddle into bottomless blackness without feeling or sound.

★ ★ ★

On high ground less than a mile away, a man dismounted and ground-hitched his horse. Moving away from his mount, he extended a brass navy telescope, pressed it to his one good eye and pointed it towards the Medicine Bow Mountains over which the sun was rising. His breathing was strained from exertion; his hands had lost their usual rock-steadiness and the telescope was jumping about. He took several deep breaths, supported his weight by resting his shoulder against the trunk of a tree, again lifted the telescope to his eye. Then, despite the sun's dazzling light causing distracting flare on the lens, he fastened onto the rider on the black horse and watched with interest as he worked his way down from the hills.

With knowledge not available to that man on the black horse, the watcher waited purposefully. And with the distant rider safely located, he risked moving the telescope a little way from his eye so that the area away to his right came into his unmagnified field of vision.

Moments later, he caught a faint, bright flash of light emanating from that area. Muzzle flash. Instantly, he clamped the telescope to his eye, again picked out the rider. As he did so, he heard the crack of a rifle from the area of the flash — and in the same instant the rider on the black horse doubled over and slowly toppled out of the saddle.

The watcher tilted the telescope fractionally downwards. Visible through a blur of obstructing scrub, the rider lay unmoving. Still watching intently, noting with satisfaction that there was no sign of any movement, the man with the telescope heard the distant drum of hoofs. Satisfied now, not bothering to wait for the new rider to come into the telescope's field of view, he took it away from his eye, contracted the brass body and slipped it into a saddle-bag.

Then, after pausing for an instant to lift the black patch away from his face and gently massage the empty eye socket, he mounted the waiting blue roan and began riding steadily north-west in the direction of Fort Steele.

★ ★ ★

Hardness digging into his back. The terrifying numbness of paralysis at his front. Difficulty in breathing. A mouth as dry as the midsummer llano.

Bywater's eyes flickered open, then snapped shut as dazzling white light seared his retina. Wherever he was, he was staring straight into the rising sun. He grunted painfully. Turned his head to one side. Slowly opened his eyes to narrow slits.

The gunman was sitting with his back against a rock, grinning as his victim struggled back to full conscious-ness. The rifle that had brought

Bywater tumbling from the saddle was cradled across his thighs. He wore a stained black Stetson, all black garb. Dark stubble covered a weak chin. His face was lined, hardened and made world-weary by a life filled with scheming and violence.

He was some thirty feet away from Bywater, separated from him by an expanse of parched grass. Lorna Doone was at the edge of the scrub, reins trailing, Bywater's gunbelt with its Colt.45 dangling from the saddlehorn.

Bywater, as his senses flooded back, realized he had been dragged off the trail and propped in a sitting position with his back against one of the grey cottonwoods — hence the hardness at his back.

The numbness . . . ? With trepidation his hand explored the front of his shirt, slid down to his belt, probed the deep dent drilled into the soft brass of the engraved buckle. Relief was instantaneous. A weight lifted from his shoulders. Suddenly he was breathing easier.

'That's where the first one hit,' the gunslinger said, watching him. 'I ain't yet decided where to put the second, but I'm damned sure it'll come to me.'

'This *was* the second,' Bywater said. 'Your first shot missed by a mile, so I'm not overly worried about the third.'

'Worry's something should be second nature to you, my friend. A Pinkerton operative is any man's meat.'

'You got the wrong information. I'm a drifter heading for the Union Pacific at Rawlins. Saratoga just happens to be in the way.'

'No. You're Temple Bywater. You left Denver three days ago, heading for Saratoga. You're operating under orders from Charlie Eames, superintendent in the Pinkerton National Detective Agency's office on the Opera House block in Denver. Tell me I'm wrong and I'll call you a liar.'

'The man you spoke to is wrong. He's the liar. From what I've heard of the Pinkertons they've got tight security. Information like that would never

11

get out of their office. The first you'll know of a Pinkerton man is when he walks up and introduces himself.'

'So if I turn out your saddle-bags I'll find nothing? No papers? No badge?'

'Go take a look — but tread carefully. Doone doesn't take kindly to nervous strangers.'

The gunman chuckled. 'Time for that when I've picked my spot and used that third bullet, taken you into Saratoga belly-down over that fine-lookin' horse.'

'And what then? Hand my dead body over to the man who put you up to this; the man living in fear of this . . . this Bywater fellow? Because to go to these lengths he must be in considerable fear — and to attract the attention of the Pinkertons, the illegal enterprise he wants kept under wraps must be far reaching in its importance. Is that it?'

'Suppose it is? All that talk proves is I'm right and you're lying, you're a Pinkerton man just like I said.'

'No. I've already told you you're

making a mistake. But you don't believe that, so more words denying it would be a waste of breath . . . '

Bywater suddenly broke off, wincing. He leaned forward and rubbed the soft leather of his boot, comforted by the feel of swelling at his right ankle. Then he forced a pained look onto his face and gazed across at the other man.

'I guess your mind's made up. And as there's no way I can match the reward this fellow must be offering . . . '

There was no reply, and none was expected. Bywater saw that the gun-man's eyes had hardened. Sweat glistened on his face, either from the heat or from tension, or from the effort of steeling himself to commit cold-blooded murder. All that strain, Bywater thought. *Works in my favour, plays havoc with the man's reactions. And while he's looking ahead with just the one grisly chore in mind, I'm about to hit him with the unexpected.*

'Every condemned man's entitled to one last request,' he said, his voice deliberately plaintive. 'That's right, isn't it?' He caught the other man's puzzled nod and said, 'I twisted my ankle real bad when I hit the ground. It was your shot did the damage — but you know that. Now I'd like nothing more than to take off my boot, enjoy a few moments' blessed relief . . . '

He shrugged hopelessly. Without waiting for a yes or a no, he bent his right knee and drew his boot up close to his hand. Then in one smooth, practised motion, he slipped the hide-away pistol out of the supple leather, cocked the hammer and planted a bullet clean between the shocked gunman's eyes.

2

Horses and wagons were hitched both sides of the street when Temple Bywater rode into Saratoga. Shops and commercial premises were open for business, the sound of a hammer striking raw iron rang musically from an unseen blacksmith's shop, and a spray of water sparkled in the morning sunlight as a swamper walked from the saloon and emptied the contents of his bucket far out into the dust.

Bywater's approach attracted attention as soon as he swung into Main Street. Men experienced in horseflesh paused in their activities, their eyes drawn to the magnificent mare with muscles rippling under a glistening black coat. That first admiring glance was followed by a second that drew brows together in a frown, for behind the mare, at the end of a short lead

15

rope, a fine-looking gelding walked with head bowed.

Those second glances that registered shock and then a whole range of emotions were noticed with resignation by Temple Bywater. He was well aware that, even face down with ankles and wrists lashed beneath his horse's belly, the dead bushwhacker on that second horse would be recognized. If not him, then his mount. And in this small town, word would spread with the speed of a summer brush fire.

Even as those thoughts crossed his mind, he saw a man stoop and whisper to a youngster in ragged trousers, saw that boy set off in a zigzag run down the plankwalk. Like an eel slipping through swaying rushes, he threaded his way between standing onlookers, making a beeline for a solid stone building with a tin roof and barred windows. As Bywater watched, the boy charged in through the open door. Moments later he emerged, followed by a tall man buckling on a gunbelt.

The badge glittering on his vest suggested that he would be astute enough to understand where Bywater was heading; a man bringing a dead body into town would be unlikely to make for the café, or for the saloon. So the tall lawman went no further than the edge of the plankwalk outside his jail. There he ruffled the boy's hair and sent him on his way, then stood with his thumbs hooked into the gunbelt to await the arrival of the newcomer and his gruesome cargo.

The boy was still running. The lawman, Bywater guessed, had sent him on another errand. To fetch the undertaker? — or to fetch a close relative who would identify the dead man?

Behind the first lawman a second, much younger man wearing a badge had appeared in the jail's doorway, half hidden in the shadows. And suddenly a worm of unease stirred in Bywater, and for the first time he found himself considering the identity of the dead young man, wondering just who it was he had killed and the position that person had occupied in this small Wyoming town.

He was still mulling over the possibilities and their likely effect on his health when he reached the jail. He eased Doone up to the hitch rail alongside a palomino and a lean buckskin, swung out of the saddle, and with a grim smile of greeting on his face turned to face the men awaiting him. The tall lawman stepped down off the plankwalk, reached for the mare's reins with one hand and with the other rammed the muzzle of his six-gun into Bywater's ribs.

★   ★   ★

The flaking black print on the desk plaque read TOM GAINES, TOWN MARSHAL. The office was businesslike, with roll-top desk, newfangled type-writer, gun rack and an iron stove on which a blackened coffee pot bubbled.

An oblong opening in the rear wall led through to the rear of the jail — Bywater guessed there was a small block out there with a couple of bare cells.

Tom Gaines was sitting behind the desk, rocking gently in a swivel chair. The other man, in his early twenties, swarthy and with more than a little Indian in his ancestry, was staring at Bywater with hard black eyes.

'Arch,' Gaines said to him, 'I think you'd best unhitch that horse and take Gus's body over to Ringling's before his pa gets here.' Then he shook his head. 'No, change that. Wait outside for Homer Allman, tell him I'll talk to him later. Then take him with you, stay with him while he arranges his son's funeral.'

The deputy nodded to the marshal, glanced in Bywater's direction then went silently out of the office.

'Arch is my deputy,' Gaines said affably. 'He's also my son. His ma was a full-blood Shoshone; she died giving birth. Joe Ringling's the town carpenter. He knocks up a fine coffin, runs a wagon pulled by a pair of high-stepping fillies that comes in handy for funerals. In case you don't know, the man you plugged is Gus Allman. His pa's the town mayor.'

'You've calmed down. One minute I've got a pistol in my ribs, the next I'm your friend. Does that mean I'm under arrest?'

'It means I'm letting you know exactly what's going on, which is what I expect you to do for me.'

'Well, sure. But a town mayor carries a lot of weight. This one's your employer. You've sent that youngster running to him with the bad news, and I figure when he gets here you'd like to demonstrate that you're on top of your job. His boy's dead: you've got the killer behind bars.

'Have I?'

'I shot him, yes.'

'Self-defence?'

'In a manner of speaking. But you saw me bring him into town. Would a murderer do that?'

Gaines pinched his nose, took a deep breath.

'I'm in no position to tell you what a killer would or would not do,' he said, 'but right now murder is a touchy subject here in Saratoga.'

'Yes,' Bywater said, 'so I've been told.'

Gaines frowned. 'By Gus Allman?'

Bywater shook his head. 'No. That feller limited his conversation to threats.'

'Then who? I've not seen you here in town, and we're too close knit a community to allow word of our troubles to spread.'

'You know damn well the importance of this particular killing extended far beyond the town limits.' Bywater shrugged. 'What you may not know is that I came over the mountains today; left Denver three days ago.'

For a long moment there was silence. Then Gaines pushed out his lips, nodded slowly.

'Well, well,' he said softly. 'Now I wonder what mention of that town is supposed to tell me.'

Bywater's gaze was steady. 'Denver's known for the Pike's Peak gold-rush.'

'That was more than thirty years ago.'

'It made a lot of men rich. Wealth gets spread around, but wise men make sure it doesn't go away. And a man in his twenties thirty years ago would today be in his fifties. Still young enough to have ambitions. And able to afford them.'

Silence settled over the room. Deep in thought, Gaines reached for the makings and began rolling a cigarette. Bywater watched him, refused the sack of tobacco when it was extended to him, then waited patiently while the marshal fired up his quirly and sat back in his chair.

Both of them heard the background clatter of boots on the plankwalk, the murmur of voices, one of those voices suddenly raised in anger. That would be Homer Allman, Bywater supposed. Town mayor. Summoned to the jail by a kid in ragged trousers, then confronted by the shocking sight of his dead son belly-down over his own horse.

The argument continued for a few minutes. Something thumped heavily against the door, and a voice thick with emotion yelled for Gaines. Another flurry, then the disturbance abated and moved away. Voices faded. A bridle jingled and there was the sound of a horse being led away from the hitch rail and across the street.

Presently, Gaines sighed. Without looking up from a prolonged study of the glowing tip of his cigarette, he began to speak.

'You ride into town with a dead man, walk in here and start talking in riddles. You stir up memories of the past, and in the same breath suggest a link with the present. It's done deliberately, and whatever it is you're hinting at must also be linked to Saratoga — or why else would you be here?' He looked up, and his blue eyes were clear and

23

untroubled. 'I haven't yet asked you your name, but don't underestimate me: that'll come, and you've told me nothing I don't already know. What bothers me a little is how much more you know, and how you came by that information. But that's of no great concern. Because I'm better than most at reading between the lines, we come back to your mention of Denver and all becomes clear — '

'Before you say any more,' Bywater cut in, 'let's you and me go look up a man by the name of Forrest Jackson.'

Gaines grunted. 'Now why the hell doesn't that come as a surprise?'

3

Bywater and Gaines left the jail, walked down the sun drenched street to the livery barn where Bywater unsaddled Doone, left instructions with a raw-boned man called Ellery Cole for the mare's care with the ancient hostler and made sure the big black horse was comfortable in a clean stall.

Forrest Jackson, Attorney at Law, worked out of an office situated on a wide street on the other side of town. The North Platte river flowed through the centre of Saratoga. To reach the western half of the town on the other side of the river, Bywater and Gaines walked down the slope and crossed a flat bridge built from solid timber baulks. Jackson's premises were directly opposite those occupied by the carpenter and undertaker, Joe Ringling. Glancing down the street, and receiving an urgent signal from his deputy who was waiting outside Ringling's, Marshal Tom Gaines prudently took Bywater up a back alley running parallel to the lower end of Main Street. They were taking that route, he explained, to avoid possible confrontation with the grief-stricken Homer Allman.

Jackson let them in through the back door that opened directly onto the alley. He was short, straight, white-haired and dressed in a shiny black suit. Pince-nez spectacles were clamped to an impressive nose. He nodded to Gaines, glanced with a thoughtful half smile at Bywater and led the way through to his frontroom office. Sunlight from the street slanted through the window. Motes drifted lazily. Brassware and fine glass glistened. There was the rich aroma of dusty leather book-bindings, of ink and warm sealing wax.

From behind his desk, Jackson gazed benevolently on the other two men as they took seats opposite him in shadows cast by the sunlight.

'I've been expecting this man for several days, Tom,' the lawyer said, hands flat on the desk. 'If the manner of his coming caused etiquette to be forgotten, let me tell you who he is. His name's Temple Bywater' — he flicked a glance at Bywater, who nodded — 'and he's an experienced investigator with the Pinkerton National Detective Agency, working out of their Denver office.'

'That much I worked out,' Gaines said. 'And if the reasons for his being here somehow eluded me, he dropped enough hints to put me right. Again, no surprise. From the outset, I knew the killing of Andrew Stone would bring in the big boys. I expected the county sheriff, maybe a federal man — but the *Pinkertons?*'

'When a man elected senator of a brand new state gets murdered,' Bywater said, 'a covert investigation seems like the best bet. The Pinkertons were brought in *through* Jackson here, but by order of a higher authority. Unfortunately, someone got wind of it. That bushwhacker, Gus Allman, knew a sight more than you do, Marshal. What he knew died with him, but the information he had came from some-one.'

'And you're assuming that someone has to be the man behind Andrew Stone's murder?' Gaines said.

'Right. A man Gus Allman must surely have been seen with. This is a small town, so both of you probably know who I'm talking about. But I'm a newcomer, and at a disadvantage. Speed is of the essence. I need background information, and then I need that man's name and the names of other people I should talk to.'

'You'll get names, and some of them will be of men Gus Allman associated with,' Forrest Jackson said, his voice suddenly businesslike. 'Sadly, I don't think those names will give you what you need to resolve this affair.'

He reached behind him, grunting a little with effort, then glass clinked and liquid gurgled in the silence as he poured whiskey from a decanter into three crystal glasses.

★ ★ ★

'You asked for background, so let's deal with that first,' Jackson said, nursing his glass. 'Today' — he glanced at his desk calendar — 'is August the first, 1890. The United States constitution was signed three years ago, Washington's been president for eighteen months and by next year we should have a Bill of Rights — making everyone happy. Wyoming's been a state for three weeks. Frank Warren will become governor later this year. And we've got one senator.'

'All states are allowed two,' Bywater said, 'regardless of population. Every senator serves for six years.'

'Right. Wyoming's first senator lives in Cheyenne — for the life of me I can't recall his name. Andrew Stone had been elected and would have been the second, but two weeks ago he was

29

shot in the back when out in his yard behind the house. There's a solid timber outhouse. Stone was swinging an axe, splitting logs to add to the cord of wood he was setting aside for winter.'

'And he's your link to the past, which is of importance only because it explains Andrew Stone's wealth,' Tom Gaines chipped in, for Bywater's benefit. 'When prospectors found gold at Cherry Creek in 1858, Stone got caught up in the Pike's Peak goldrush. He was still there, accumulating a small fortune, when Archerson Territory became Colorado Territory in 1861 and Denver was incorporated as a city. But he was always restless, always looking for something to do with his money.'

'He waited thirty years, then found it here,' Forrest Jackson said. 'He heard about the hot springs in these parts, and was one of the first whites to move in after smallpox drove away the Indians. He was in at the beginning, when Saratoga was established — that was around 1878 — and, ever since, he's been making the place cosy for miners from the Sierras, visitors from as far away as England.'

Bywater sipped his whiskey. 'He married?'

'Left a young widow. A young woman from a poor background.'

'And now she's rich.'

'You betcha.'

'And yes, that could be a motive for murder,' Tom Gaines said, 'though if Elizabeth was after his cash she would have needed help. But that's nonsense; as far as I'm aware, she was devoted to her husband.' He hesitated. 'It's also possible Stone made enemies in his gold-rush days and those men tracked him down and came a-hunting. But the passage of so much time makes that unlikely; my money's on the man who came a close second to Stone in that election.'

'Let me guess,' Bywater said. 'That would be Homer Allman, mayor of this town. The man whose son shot me out of the saddle with a Winchester rifle.'

'Nice try, but wrong,' Forrest Jackson said — then blinked. 'Did he really do that?'

Bywater nodded. 'So if Allman wasn't the man who had his ambitions thwarted, why the hell would he want me dead.'

'Maybe he doesn't. Maybe someone else was paying his son.'

'And that brings us to Nathan Wedge,' Gaines said. 'He's the man who lost out in that election by a couple of hundred votes, demanded a recount, and was shocked to see his shortfall increase.'

All three men sipped their drinks, lost in thought as silence settled over the room. Temple Bywater had listened with interest to everything that had been said, but had heard nothing that pointed to Andrew Stone's killer. Nathan Wedge had such a strong motive, obvious to everyone, it virtually ruled him out; ordering Stone's murder would be as good as slipping his own neck in the hangman's noose. Homer

Allman's son had tried to kill Bywater, and might have been in the pay of Stone's killer — but Gus Allman was dead. Stone might have been murdered so that the killer could get to his wealth through his pretty widow, but that was a long shot. As was an enemy from the past.

Tom Gaines was watching him.

'As town marshal I've got my own investigation going, but I'd appreciate any help you can give me,' he said quietly. 'Talking to us was a start, and I guess your next step will be to go wet your whistle in the saloon, listen to Ike Adams.' He flashed a look at Jackson. 'If anything's been said in this town, you can bet your bottom dollar Ike's heard it, and remembers — though much of what he says should be taken with a big pinch of salt.'

'I'll bear that in mind,' Bywater said. 'But talking to you two wasn't a start, it was a waste of time: neither of you has given me the information I requested.' He watched Jackson, saw the slight lowering of the head, the thoughtful narrowing of the eyes. 'I want the name of that one eminent person Gus Allman *must* have associated with. You're both residents of this town. You must know him, and know him well. And he's a clever bastard. Somehow, that man found out what Charlie Eames was planning up in the Pinkerton's Denver office, and he sent Allman out to intercept me. I can see only one reason for doing that: he has something to hide. That something can only be the murder of Andrew Stone.'

Jackson flashed a glance at the marshal, and when Tom Gaines shrugged and looked at Bywater his manner were strangely guarded.

'The obvious name,' he said, 'is Nathan Wedge, the beaten candidate.'

'As runner up, does he automatically get elected in Stone's place?'

'The finer points of the political processes elude me, but I know he's got the right man backing him.'

'Bradley Wynne.' Behind the desk,

Jackson spread his hands. 'Don't worry about the name, or the man's position. He has no relevance other than his immense wealth and influence and the fact that he's solidly behind Nathan Wedge. Wedge is a married man, a respected member of the community. He's manager of the bank here in Saratoga, and assists regularly in the Forte Steele bank. Been going there a couple of times a month for the past year. So, yes, I can't see anything standing in the way of his getting elected in place of the deceased Andrew Stone.'

Bywater nodded. 'But there's no second election?'

'Oh no. The names of qualified and eminently suitable men are brought forward, and considered. There are delib-erations. A decision will be reached . . . ' Jackson shrugged.

'Days, weeks?'

'At any time. A matter of days, or less.'

'Yeah, that's all straightforward enough,'

Gaines said. 'But what I was about to point out was that although Wedge is the obvious suspect, Gus Allman never got close to him.'

'The two moved in different circles?' Jackson said.

'Right.' Gaines nodded. 'If Allman did gun down Andrew Stone at Wedge's behest, they met in secret.'

Jackson was pushing his lips forward, deep in thought.

'Gus lived at home with his pa,' he said slowly. 'As town mayor, Homer Allman *did* have frequent meetings with Wedge. It's possible the killing could have been arranged that way.'

Gaines shook his head. 'That would put Homer in up to his neck, and I just can't see it.'

Bywater lifted an eyebrow. 'You don't think he's involved?'

'He's town mayor, a top job. That's a lot to put on the line.'

'But there would be a lot to gain if he helped a wealthy man into the US Senate.' Bywater took a deep breath.

'So, what about that name?' He waited, got no reaction. 'Christ,' he said, 'this is like pulling teeth from a man with his mouth tight shut.'

That brought a grin from Tom Gaines. Then he shook his head.

'Forrest warned you that naming names might not give you what you need. That's because Gus Allman was an ex-con who left prison six months ago after a five-year-term for armed robbery. He went straight back to his old ways, mixing with gunslingers, hellions, local riff-raff. He did not mix, or talk to, men of standing in this town. If you want names, I can give you Hank Geary and Parker Laing. They were Allman's close buddies — but they're gunslingers. They don't hire men to do their killing; they get hired: if the cash is right, they'd be more than happy to point the gun, pull the trigger.'

'So, for a price, they could replace Gus Allman. Which means I'm still in danger.'

'You were in danger as soon as you

37

were pegged as a Pinkerton operative — you know that.'

'And that's it? You can't give me the man who hired Allman?'

'That hiring must have been done in secret. The only time I recall Gus Allman talking to a man of authority,' Gaines said firmly, 'was when he stood up in court and cursed the judge who sent him to jail.'

★   ★   ★

Bywater had gone. Jackson had left his desk to draw the curtains. He and Tom Gaines were sitting in brooding silence, sipping whiskey.

'You weren't exactly straight with him,' Gaines said at last.

Jackson's chuckle was dry.

'I like that 'not exactly'. I wasn't straight with him, period. The man got nothing he didn't already know, left here — I hope — without a flicker of suspicion.'

'But he will find out.'

'Bound to.'

'So — what then?'

'I agreed that he'd find out. The question is, when? — and the answer to that will give you the answer to your question: 'what then?'.'

Gaines nodded thoughtfully.

'The later the better — right?'

'I would say so.'

'And to that end, delaying tactics will be used?'

'You talk like a weasel, Tom,' Jackson said, crystal sparkling in the gloom as he lifted the glass to his thin lips. 'Bywater will be stopped.'

'Yeah, I thought that's what you'd say,' the town marshal said gloomily.

4

It was close to midday when Bywater left the lawman and the lawyer in Forrest Jackson's office and made his way back across the river to the east side of town. He recalled passing the saloon as he rode in with Gus Allman's dead body, and considered going there at once. But he also recalled eating breakfast early up in the hills, and was at once aware of a sound in his belly like the warning rumble of a distant stampede. He looked about him. There was a café alongside the town's only hotel. The cow-bell hanging above the door clanked as he entered an atmosphere of smoke and grease and ordered beef-steak, eggs and coffee from a man in a grubby apron. Thirty minutes later, sitting back in his chair, he finished off the meal with a second cup of black java and a leisurely cigarette.

40

Then he strode across the street and up the slope to talk to Ike Adams.

Behind a rickety false front the saloon's only room was big, cool and host to a handful of drinkers. Bywater's boots swished through the thin layer of sawdust scattered across the board floor as he walked towards the bar. He was aware of a sudden unnatural silence, of two men watching him from the gloom. A glance in their direction revealed sprawled arrogance, stained, drab clothing, the glint of dark eyes and the gleam of metal deliberately displayed in tied-down thigh holsters.

Bywater let them know they'd been spotted, then turned away and walked up to a bar that was at least twenty feet long. Behind it a tall man with a face like weathered oak split by time was polishing a glass with a surprisingly white cloth and watching him with interest.

'Well if it isn't the Pinkerton detective,' he said.

He set the glass down, filled it with

warm beer from a tall jug, stepped back with his arms folded.

Bywater set a coin ringing on the bar.

'Does everyone know,' he said, 'or is it just you?'

'They know,' the tall man said, and he nodded towards the two rough-looking gents who had left their table and were walking lazily towards the door with spurs jingling. 'That's something that should concern you mightily.'

'Hank Geary and Parker Laing,' Bywater said. 'At a guess. And you must be Ike Adams.'

'Keep guessing like that,' Adams said, 'and you'll have this case solved by sundown.' He looked across the room, watched the two men as they walked out into the bright sunlight. 'Geary's the skinny feller with the floppy hat, blond hair. That makes the dark, stocky one Laing. Both bad eggs. Neither of them are locals. Far as I know they got acquainted with Gus Allman in the state pen, followed his dust when he washed the prison stink off his pale skin and headed home. They've been hanging around ever since.'

'In terms of information freely given, my visit here's already paying off,' Bywater said, grinning.

He extended a hand. The two men shook.

'Guesswork's another name for luck,' Bywater said, 'and it's not much use without help and backup. I'm told you're a good listener with one hell of a memory.'

'Michael Carey at the general store is another good bet. Down the street from Cole's livery barn. Most people in town buy supplies there. Take their time over it, too, do a lot of talking.'

'I'll try him another time,' Bywater said, waiting.

'Well, noon's always a slack time here, so you're in luck,' Adams said, glancing at the men lolling against the bar. 'Let's you and me slip away, take a seat and talk turkey.'

He picked up the jug and another glass and led the way to a table near a battered piano with yellowed keys. Adams topped up Bywater's glass, filled his own. As they settled, a white-haired old man in tattered denim trousers and a cowhide vest over a naked upper torso that was skin and bone carried a glass unsteadily over to the piano, sat down and began tinkling the ivories. A honky-tonk melody plinked out discordantly. The remaining two customers hastily downed their drinks and left.

'Never fails,' Adams said. 'That's Old Man Stoker. I should hire him for times of trouble.'

'Are there any other times?' Bywater said, and Adams chuckled.

'This town's been in white hands for less than fifteen years,' he said. 'Worst that's happened in that time is the murder of Andrew Stone less than a month ago. Second worst would have been the death of one Temple Bywater, Pinkerton man — only that didn't happen, because Gus Allman had been misinformed: you proved to be a mite tougher than he'd expected.'

'Misinformed by whom?'

Adams looked him in the eye. 'Is this where your guesswork needs help?'

'Gus Allman knew the Pinkertons were about to become involved, but how did he find out? According to Tom Gaines and Forrest Jackson — two men who should know — Allman was a gunman who mixed only with his own kind.'

'Those that know,' Adams said, 'don't always tell.'

'Why not?'

'Any Pinkerton man worth his salt could work that one out — and he wouldn't need to guess.'

'Don't tell me they're involved in Stone's murder. I've just left them. Gaines comes across as straight. Forrest Jackson's a respected lawyer.'

'Maybe not involved directly, or knowingly, but didn't I hear somewhere that Jackson was the middle man, the link between Washington and Denver when Pinkerton involvement was being discussed? If he was, who better to pass on that information? — to the wrong people, deliberately or accidentally, take your pick.'

Bywater frowned. 'I can see him taking Tom Gaines into his confidence. But it seems he didn't, because Gaines wasn't expecting the Pinkertons. So if Jackson kept the town marshal in the dark, why would he talk to a desperado like Gus Allman?'

'You're too trusting,' Adams said, 'and trust is an honour not bestowed, but hard-earned. Forrest Jackson's brother, Millard — '

'Millard Jackson?'

'That's right. Why?'

'I'm not sure. Let's just say the name set bells ringing. They were there, but muted, when I was talking to Forrest. But mention of Millard's really set them off. It'll come to me . . . But go on, you were saying?'

'Yeah, well, Millard Jackson was Gus Allman's lawyer. He defended Allman against a charge of armed robbery, and lost. Allman did five years. When he rode back into town, Forrest Jackson was the first man he looked up. They've been meeting off and on ever since.'

★   ★   ★

When Bywater stepped from the saloon into the blistering heat of the day his first instinct was to look about him. Marshal Gaines had given him Geary and Laing, saloonist Ike Adams had as good as told him those men were dangerous and warned him to watch his back. All right, it was early afternoon and broad daylight, but that wouldn't deter hardcases being paid good cash to do a job. And a busy street could be the ideal place to fire a fatal shot and melt away into the dust and the heat.

So Bywater stepped back into the shadow of the saloon's overhang, looked up and down the street, and at once caught sight of Geary and Laing. They were across the street, slouching with elbows resting on the hitch rail outside the hotel as they talked to a man with dark hair greying at the temples. His spare frame was haughtily upright, set off by expensive clothing and tooled leather boots into which dovegrey pants were tucked. A vain man, Bywater judged, probably from necessity because he was out to impress. So, was he Nathan Wedge?

As if sensing Bywater's gaze, and his question, the man glanced across the street. He smiled dismissively, then clapped Parker Laing on the shoulder and limped away into the hotel.

The two gunslingers ambled off, Laing casting the occasional glance over his shoulder. Watching me, Bywater thought. Waiting to see what I do, where I go.

Then, shaking his head, he dismissed all three men from his mind as he rolled a cigarette and worked out the details of his next move.

Gus Allman had been sent out to eliminate the Pinkerton man, which had given credence to Bywater's nagging worries of the previous night.

However, despite Allman's ambush, he had made it to Saratoga. Once in town he had listened but learned nothing he did not already know: the newly elected senator of the State of Wyoming had been shot dead in his own back yard, and his killer was still at large. Anything else had to be taken at face value because, if Ike Adams was to be believed, the men Bywater thought to be honest had been deliberately lying.

Now, with the sun past its meridian, it was time to take the investigation a step further. Charlie Eames over in the Pinkerton's Denver office was a shrewd organizer who believed in covering every eventuality. The news of the Pinkerton's involvement had certainly reached Saratoga before Bywater, but those waiting for it had got only got half the story. Bywater was determined that, for as long as it was possible, the second half should remain a secret.

Within the next hour, he would be riding south from Saratoga. Before he set off, he needed a reason for his trip that was valid, but not the real one. The man to see was Marshal Tom Gaines.

★   ★   ★

The jail's office was unchanged, but there was a subtle difference in the town marshal's manner. He knows he lied, Bywater thought. He must realize I've discovered his mendacity. Well, now's his chance to make up for it.

Gaines was in his swivel chair, smoking a cigarette, booted feet on the desk. There was no sign of the big deputy, Jack Bright. Gaines gestured to a chair. Bywater spun it in his hands, straddled it, leaned on the back — and waited.

Uneasily, Gaines said, 'You talk to Adams?'

'At length. And you were right. He's a fount of knowledge. Listening to him was like eavesdropping on secret conversations.'

'Good, good.' Gaines nodded, his eyes unreadable. 'So, what next? If you're set on interviewing suspects, I can point you in the right direction.'

'Well, I do need to talk to Homer Allman, Nathan Wedge, and Andrew Stone's widow. But today I feel like riding south along the river. I was told in Denver there's an old-timer lives down that way, keeps himself to himself, been down there for years.'

'Homer Allman and his wife were taken to Rawlins where they boarded a train East to be with their folks. As for the old-timer, yes, you're right. You'll find him ten miles downriver, halfway between here and Riverside.'

Bywater nodded, hiding his satisfaction. 'Just to make sure we're talking about the same fellow, this old-timer goes by the name Logan?'

'Yep. Texas Jack Logan.' Gaines smiled, a noticeable relaxation in his demeanour as the conversation seemed to be proceeding without confrontation. 'He's another veteran of the Pike's Peak gold-rush, though I'm pretty sure he's never met Andrew Stone. Lives in a riverside shack. Keeps an American Arms 12-guage to deter marauders.'

'That would certainly do the job,' Bywater said, nodding. 'I'll make sure I'm whistling when I ride in.'

'He's hard of hearing,' Gaines said. 'Circle around, come in from the river so he can see you — and keep your hands in sight.'

'That's Logan sorted out,' Bywater said. 'What about Geary and Laing?'

Gaines frowned. 'What about them?'

'Our paths crossed in Ike Adams's place. They've been keeping their eye on me. I'd like to ride south with eyes front, not watching my back trail. Maybe your boy could keep an eye on them, step in and dissuade them if they look like following me.'

Gaines pulled a face. 'I'd like to oblige, but there's no law against a man leaving town.' He forced a grin. 'Pity nobody's written a law forcing them out, but until they do something wrong — '

'There's nothing you can do,' Bywater

finished for him.

He slid the chair out from under him, spun, and made for the door. There, he turned.

'Thanks for your help, Marshal,' he said, straightfaced. 'Oh, and isn't there a little something you forgot to mention when we were talking this morning?'

Gaines went still, suddenly wary.

'What's that?'

'Geary and Laing are real friendly with a man I'm pretty sure is the politician, Nathan Wedge,' Bywater said. 'Now why would an ambitious man with his eyes set on power be consorting with ex-cons? — and does the marshal of Saratoga already know about this, or has it come as a complete surprise?'

His words went unanswered. Touching the brim of his hat with his forefinger, Bywater walked out into the street leaving behind him a strained silence. He mulled over that negative reaction as he walked across to the livery barn, but when he'd finished saddling Doone, checked his Colt .45 and '73 Winchester and filled his water bottle from the pump outside the barn, he was still no closer to clarifying his thoughts or answering his own questions.

Had his remark to Tom Gaines about Nathan Wedge's hoodlum associates evoked genuine shock, or had he struck a raw nerve that left the marshal exposed to accusations of connivance, and Bywater in even greater danger?

★ ★ ★

When Temple Bywater walked out of the jail office and climbed aboard Doone, Nathan Wedge was inside the hotel lounge and looking far from confident. Hank Geary and Parker Laing were stretched out in shabby easy chairs, Stetsons pushed back, drinks held in their gloved hands. Wedge was puffing on a cigar, and pacing restlessly.

'Damn,' he said, coming to a halt in front of the two gunmen. 'And double damn that fool Gus Allman. Early morning, a clear day . . . and he bungles the job.'

'Whoever it was sent him out after that Pinkerton man,' Geary said, 'he sure didn't check on that boy's record.'

'What does that mean?' Wedge said.

'That boy couldn't shoot himself in the foot if he held the muzzle tight up against it,' Geary said, and Laing chuckled.

'Now me and Parker there,' he said, 'can guarantee to get rid of the Pinkerton man for you — if that's what you want.'

'It's not,' Wedge said. Then he shook his head irritably. 'Hell, I don't know *what* I want. All I know for sure is if that Pinkerton operative digs too deep, all my plans come to naught, and I'm finished.'

He'd begun pacing again. His restlessness had carried him to the window. From there he could see the jail. Without turning, he said, 'Bywater's riding out.'

'Then he's playin' into your hands,' Geary said approvingly. 'Once he's out where the buzzards fly, there's nothing to stop us. First option is to get ahold of him and beat some sense into the sucker. Point him back to Denver and — '

'Why waste all that energy?' Laing protested. 'Takes less effort to pull a Winchester's trigger. And I tell you, I ain't no Gus Allman.'

'I've hired you for the day,' Wedge said, 'and up to now you've done nothing to earn that money. Get your horses. We'll follow Bywater.'

'Yeah?' Geary said, climbing lazily to his feet. 'I like it — but what's it to be? Knock some sense into him, or hang back and place a bullet in the back of his skull?'

'Neither, if I can avoid it,' Wedge said. 'If I can talk my way out of this . . . give him something . . . ' He looked from Geary to Laing. 'But that may not be possible. Bring your rifles, both of you — and get a move on.'

And with that he turned on his heel and stormed out of the hotel.

5

A summer storm was gathering its forces over the 12,000-foot Medicine Bow Peak when Bywater rode out of town, the skies away to the east purple and swollen and riven by jagged threads of lightning. The air was hot and still and, even though Bywater maintained an even pace, the big black mare was soon lathered and breathing hard. Riding close to the cool waters of the North Platte gave horse and rider some relief, but regular glances over his left shoulder told Bywater that the solace that would come with the drenching rains of the breaking storm was still more than an hour away.

Before he had ridden five miles towards Texas Jack Logan's riverside home, those same backward glances also told him that he was not alone. The knowledge came as no surprise. The fact that there were three men shadowing him gave Bywater food for thought. He had expected Geary and Laing, but who was the third man?

Letting that thought linger in his subconscious he pushed on steadily, his slight but understandable uneasiness allayed by the favourable conditions. He had no difficulty with visibility: the terrain was undulating but never rugged, and most of the trees clung to the river-bank making it difficult for pursuers to close in without being seen. Also, apart from the comfortable beat of his horse's hoofs, there was nothing to impede his hearing: the North Platte seemed muted by the approaching bad weather, its flattened waters the dull colour of lead as they flowed steadily north on their long, sweeping journey to the Missouri.

Watching, listening, always mindful that less than twelve hours ago a rifle bullet had almost ended his life, Bywater rode south. He took advantage of what little cover was available — for much of the way that drove him off the trail to work his mount through the North Platte's fringe of cottonwoods. Once he drew rein and sat smoking a cigarette, and a thin smile twitched his lips as he watched three riders crest a low rise less than a mile back and pull up to sit motionless with the purple skies at their backs.

Then, another half-hour on, as the skies overhead darkened and the wind picked up and the first heavy spots of rain came driving like buckshot out of the east, his journey was over. He rode out of the trees on one of the North Platte's long curves and ahead of him a squat cabin, its shingle roof already wet and glistening, was set back in a stand of quaking aspens some fifty yards from the North Platte.

Come in from the river, Tom Gaines had said. Cautiously, Bywater followed the trees along the riverbank until he could turn and approach the cabin from the front. He wheeled the big black horse. Branches were rattling in the wind as he rode up the slight slope, the rain hissing across the grass. In the gathering gloom, a light was visible, glowing in one of the cabin's windows. Under a rickety overhang, the gallery was empty. His head half turned away from the driving rain, Bywater could see a buckboard in an open barn, several horses standing miserably at one end of a small pole corral.

Suddenly the cabin's door burst open, the crash as it hit the log walls lost in the fury of the storm. Outlined against the lamplight, a huge man appeared. He was holding a shotgun. Bywater saw his mouth open in a soundless shout, saw the gun lift and point in his direction. Then, with a hiss and a smell of ozone, lightning flashed overhead. It was followed almost immediately by a crack of thunder.

Blinded, deafened, Bywater sat in torrential rain and waited to be cut in two.

★ ★ ★

'There are three men out there,' Bywater said, 'less than a mile behind me. This storm will hold them for a while, but they're after something and sooner or later they'll make a move.'

'So we wait.'

This was the big man. Texas Jack Logan was an ex-Pinkerton operative and an old friend, who had retired and moved north to Wyoming Territory. Bywater knew for a fact that the hearing problems mentioned by Marshal Gaines were exaggerated by the old-timer so that in some situations he had a sneaking advantage. He was solid and bearded, his hair like sun-bleached prairie grass flattened by prevailing winds. Blue eyes glittered as he made the no-nonsense pronouncement. The American Arms 12-gauge that had been lowered when Bywater hoarsely identified himself now rested against the table, within reach of Logan's enormous paw. A huge .44 jutted from a holster set high on his hip.

Across the table another man, tall and wiry, as dark as a hickory pole, was watching and listening with amusement. Clarence 'Bony' Sugg, Bywater's long time Pinkerton partner, took very little seriously. He'd left Denver on the same day as Bywater, ridden with him as far as Albany then cut west through the mountains on his way to Texas Jack's cabin. He was the second half of the Pinkerton story Bywater wanted kept secret: two operatives, one of them undercover, Sugg being the hole card that was only of value while remaining unseen by the opposition.

Bywater was standing with his back to the iron stove. His damp clothes were steaming. He was idly looking around the room. In the shadows beyond the stove, Logan's cot was covered in animal skins. A small board on which a short rock-chipping hammer was mounted hung on the wall above it. A metal plate with an engraved inscription was attached to the board below the hammer's wooden haft.

He saw Sugg watching him, and winked. 'Those three out there, they've got me puzzled,' he said, clasping a hot coffee cup in both hands. 'I'd lay odds on two being Hank Geary and Parker Laing, two ex-cons. The man I saw them talking to in town was Nathan Wedge — I think. The odds are shorter, but I reckon he's the third.'

Sugg grunted. 'If I recall Charlie Eames's briefing back in Denver, Wedge is the defeated candidate. If he was behind the murder of Andrew Stone, the man who got elected, he'll want you out of the way. But openly riding with two jail birds? Wouldn't that be risky?'

'If I'm dead, who's going to talk?'

'Yeah, but if that was the intention, why ride ten miles and do nothing? One aimed shot from a distance, and you'd've been dead meat.'

'With you out of the way,' Texas Jack said in a voice like a pickaxe chipping at rock, 'Wedge could rest easy. But no man gets to be senator without some intelligence, so he'll be looking at complications, wondering if you're working solo or with a partner. Maybe the object of the exercise is not to take life, but to gather information. Easy enough for him to find out where you were heading — you discussed it with Tom Gaines. Just as easy to dream up a dozen valid reasons why he and his henchmen are riding in the same direction. Then along comes the storm, and now he's got a reason for seeking shelter.' The big man grinned. 'I told you we'd wait, and now I know what we're waiting for. You mark my words, any minute now you'll hear a horse whinnying out there in the rain and a miserable, bedraggled Nathan Wedge'll come a-knocking on that door.'

*   *   *

Texas Jack Logan was right in every respect other than Nathan Wedge's appearance and demeanour. The men waiting in the cabin did hear a horse whinny, and it was followed by an insistent pounding on the door. But when Wedge strode into the cabin,

64

soaked to the skin and with the wind and rain buffeting his back, the look in his penetrating dark eyes told those awaiting his arrival that here was a man of steely disposition, and he was on a mission.

That was nothing less than Bywater had expected. But for Wedge to burst in alone and, seemingly, unarmed, suggested the purpose of his ride south was not to rid himself of an annoying Pinkerton operative. But if that wasn't it — then what was going on?

With a quick glance at Sugg, Bywater proceeded to find out.

'Nathan Wedge?'

The newcomer nodded curtly.

'Is this the prelude to something more serious? Like, weighing up the strength of the opposition before calling in your two pet gunmen?'

Wedge whipped off his hat, sent rainwater cascading across the dirt floor as he slapped it against his dove-grey pants. An amused smile twitched his lips.

'There is something a damned sight

more serious in the offing, my friend, but it has very little to do with my two good friends. Laing and Geary are there to watch my back. At the moment they're finding what shelter they can under the trees, while still keeping their eyes skinned.'

'I'm sure you know my name, and why I'm in Saratoga.' Bywater watched Wedge dip his head, and went on, 'The man who murdered Andrew Stone must be looking on that as a job well done. Why would he now go after you? Are you next in line for the senatorship?'

'Yes, I am,' Wedge said, 'and, for the record, I had nothing to do with the murder of Andrew Stone.'

'All right, so what's this something a damned sight more serious that's in the offing?' Bywater said.

Wedge looked at his waterlogged Stetson, placed it brim down on the table, and met Bywater's eyes.

'Another man,' he said, 'has come forward to bid for the senatorship.'

'The hell you say,' Bywater said

softly, immediately thinking of Homer Allman, and his own suggestion that the ambitious mayor might throw his hat in the ring. 'Are you saying this other fellow's crawled out of the Saratoga woodwork to bid for the senatorship?'

'Not exactly.'

'Then what — exactly?'

'He's making his bid, but to say he's crawled out of the woodwork is to ignore his reputation. Also, it could be the Pinkertons have slipped up. Saratoga's the centre of an investigation because that's where Andrew Stone was murdered. But this new contender in the race for the second senatorship lives some thirty miles upriver in Fort Steele. It's possible you're looking for your killer in the wrong town.'

★ ★ ★

'Has this man got a name?'

The amusement was back in Wedge's eyes.

'Isn't that something you should have

learned from the two men you spent time with this morning — or at least from the lawyer who helped arrange your presence in Saratoga?'

'Not if the new contender's only recently emerged.'

'Pah!' Wedge's exclamation was derisory. 'Jackson's a lawyer, it's his job to know exactly what's going on. And Tom Gaines was talking to Kerrigan, the Fort Steele marshal, only last week.'

'All right,' Bywater said blandly, 'that's those two put in their place, but what about you? You've followed me ten miles through a rainstorm to deliver bad news. Why go to all that trouble? You could have crossed the street and spoken to me in Saratoga.'

'Because politics is a dirty game. Stone was murdered because he won an election. I'm next in line. If the killing was politically motivated — and, by God, it must have been — that puts me in danger. I don't want to make things worse by being seen talking to the Pinkertons.'

Jack Logan left the table, crossed to the stove and stepped around Bywater. A tin pot clattered, liquid gurgled, and he returned to the table carrying four steaming tin cups. Wedge nodded his thanks and sat down. Bywater picked up a cup then went back to the stove to let the heat continue its work on his damp clothes.

'That's one possibility,' he said to Wedge, 'but you said yourself, politics is a dirty game. Dropping another suspect in my lap could be you buying yourself time.'

For the first time, Clarence Sugg stretched his long frame in the hard chair and joined the conversation.

'Why did this new *hombre* hang back until Stone was out of it? Why decide to come in when you're in line for the job?'

'Maybe he was a Stone supporter,' Bywater said, pre-empting Wedge's reply; and even as he spoke he was following that thought to its logical conclusion. 'There's one hell of a rush on: two senators are needed, and pretty damn quick. Maybe this man believes the quickest way of stopping Mr Wedge here is to get elected in his place.'

Wedge shook his head. 'You know damn well that's not the reason I'm paying Hank Geary and Parker Laing good money to watch my back for a day.'

'No,' Bywater acknowledged. 'You believe this man could be behind the Stone killing, and that puts you in danger.' He thought for a moment, pounced on another obvious objection. 'I've got to confess to ignorance of the political processes involved here,' he said, 'but I can't understand how a man can be a nobody one day, a potential United States senator the next. So what's he got going for him, this new fellow? Is reputation and standing enough at this late stage?'

'He's got money,' Nathan Wedge said, with a cynical twist to his lips. 'Reputation is fine, but because politics is a dirty game, money talks — and this man has it in abundance.'

'And he's not the only one.'

Wedge cocked his head. 'What does that mean?'

'Come on. You've got a wealthy backer. That not only oils the wheels, it means — if he's been there from the start — there's someone else out there who could be behind Stone's killing.'

'Bradley Wynne?' Wedge's eyes had widened in amazement. 'Money, yes, backing me, maybe, but if you believe he'd be party to murder, you just don't know the man.'

Texas Jack Logan had tired of the talk and now he left the table, muttering something into his beard about attending to his traps. He opened the cabin's door and stepped outside, letting in a flood of bright sunlight. The rain had stopped, the wind had died away and the heat was lifting a thin mist from saturated ground all the way down to the river. Bywater heard Logan's footsteps clattering on the gallery, followed by the soft squelch of wet earth, and guessed he was making his way to the corral.

Nathan Wedge placed his empty cup on the table, climbed to his feet and stretched.

'This discussion's taken on the nature of farce, and it's high time I left,' he said. 'I've done what I considered to be my duty. What you do next is up to you. But one thread of truth has been visible throughout our talk: I'm in line for the senatorship, and that puts me in danger. So what I would like you to do is use the information I've given you, if you must, but leave me out of it; forget where and when you heard about this new candidate.'

He waited. Bywater shook his head.

'Give me the name, and my memory will dim.'

'Go back to your lawyer. Ask him.'

'No.'

Wedge smiled enigmatically. 'Why not? Don't you trust him?'

'I'd like something more from you than rumour. Give me something to work with.'

'The man I'm talking about is also a lawyer. I told you he works out of Fort Steele, but he has close connections with Saratoga.' He paused, watching Bywater. 'Are you getting an idea of where this is going, or do you need more?'

'Finish what you started.'

'All right. His name is Millard Jackson.' Wedge nodded. 'Yes, that's right. The new man aiming to be senator is Forrest Jackson's brother.'

6

With Wedge gone and Texas Jack Logan away upriver attending to traps, the two Pinkerton operatives had the cabin to themselves. Bywater made good use of the solitude by bringing Clarence Sugg up to date with his progress, which took no time at all: he had been in Saratoga less than a day, and if he had learned anything it was that an apparently simple murder investigation had begun with a bushwhacking and was developing an impressive list of complications.

Complications were always best dealt with one at a time. The two men decided that Bywater would head straight for Fort Steele and talk to Millard Jackson. Sugg would remain in Logan's cabin that night, but would ride in to Saratoga the next day and play the drifter while mooching around town with eyes and ears open.

When they were just about finished, Bywater remembered the way Millard Jackson's name had touched a chord in his memory without playing the full tune, and he asked Sugg if he could come up with anything.

'If we're talking politics,' Sugg said, 'the only Jackson I can recall is the man who shot Joseph Goodbread in Shelby County, Texas. That touched off a four year war. Remember those vigilantes, the Regulators?'

Bywater did, though it was all well before his time. And the Jackson who fired the shot was Charles, not Millard.

★   ★   ★

It was late afternoon when Temple Bywater left the cabin by the river. The bullet that had bruised his belly was keeping that morning's bushwhacking strong in his mind, and he was well aware that Nathan Wedge and his two bodyguards, with their rifles, could be lurking in the woods.

Before riding off he took some time to study the woods behind the cabin, the hoofprints in the soft ground in front of it. The heavy rain had washed away all signs of earlier activity but, after walking out of the cabin, Wedge had unhitched his horse and left under clear skies. Bywater followed the tracks of that single horse for half a mile. There he saw in the mud clear signs of two more horses cantering down at an angle from the woods. All three horses came together on the trail, and headed north.

Bywater turned away, reasonably satisfied. If danger lay ahead, it was unlikely to come from Wedge, Geary or Laing, who were almost certainly heading back to Saratoga.

Nevertheless, because of the possibility of danger from another source, the North Platte and the shelter afforded by the ever-present cottonwoods again beckoned as the safest place to ride. Bywater eased Doone down to the river's east bank, and lightly touched the mare's ribs with his heels.

The skies overhead were still clear but, away to the east, thunder clouds were massing with frightening speed. Already the light was moving through the spectrum to an eerie yellow, and the scent of rain was in the air.

Bywater was heading downstream. Despite moving over ground made soggy by the heavy rain, Doone was soon making good time. But, thinking ahead, it didn't take long for Bywater to realize that the plans he had made with Sugg were badly flawed. A thirty mile ride to Fort Steele would see him arriving long after the town's business premises had closed. By the time Bywater got there, lawyer Millard Jackson would be at home with his feet up.

Acknowledging that little could be done that night, Bywater continued riding north but with the new intention of returning to Saratoga. He would book into the hotel, eat in its restaurant, cross the street to see if Ike Adams had heard any interesting whispers and share a drink with the amiable saloonist before retiring to bed.

And he had a half-smile on his face, anticipating an agreeable evening, when Doone abruptly pulled up and swung side-on, snorting. When Bywater looked up he was confronted by a rider blocking the way ahead.

The man was mounted on a black horse. His pale skin was emphasized by a dusty black outfit, and the black patch over his left eye. He was carrying what Bywater recognized as a Henry .44 rifle. It was pointing at Bywater's already damaged belt buckle.

'Goddamn,' he said softly.

'It's a bitch,' the man agreed.

'Are you Gus Allman's replacement?'

'You could say.'

'I learned his name when he was dead. I'd hate for the same to happen here.'

'Don't count on it. My name is Floyd Loomis. I've heard they call me Grave. So now you know — but what good will it do you?'

'Grave Loomis.' Bywater nodded. 'And you're being paid by the man who arranged Andrew Stone's murder.'

'Being paid, yes. But the man who's forking out the cash, and his reasons for doing it, have got nothing to do with the killing of Andrew Stone.'

'Bull! I'm investigating a crime. Gus Allman tried to keep me out of Saratoga, and failed. Now you're having a shot at it.'

Bywater's choice of words seemed to amuse the man with the Henry rifle. He grinned, shook his head.

'It'll surely come to that if you take the hard way out.' His gloved hand slid lovingly along the rifle's barrel. 'This has got nothing to do with Andrew Stone — but that's no longer your concern. You're out of it, and the easy way is to turn around now and head back to Denver.'

'That won't happen until I've found Stone's killer.'

Absently, keeping his eyes deliberately unfocused, Bywater let his gaze drift over Loomis's shoulder. He watched a big man step out of the trees fifty yards downstream. The man was bearded. He was carrying a shotgun. In the eerie yellow light he looked like a massive, golden-haired bear. As he moved silently towards Floyd Loomis, the first hard spots of rain began falling. Lightning flashed. In the distance, thunder rumbled.

'But you never know,' Bywater said, returning his gaze to Loomis's single eye. 'Could be the other way around, and Stone's killer has found me.'

Loomis chuckled.

'Wrong again. But that's of no account. It's time you turned that black mare around and pointed her nose towards Colorado.'

'No. It's time you took a look over your shoulder, then put down that rifle.'

Loomis shook his head. 'A Pinkerton man, using the oldest trick in the book? You disappoint me, feller. I was expecting trickery, misdirection, a good stab at a fast draw when my attention

80

wandered, but not that hoary old — '

'You should have listened to the man, let your attention wander,' a gravelly voice cut in.

Loomis froze. Bywater watched his good eye become speculative, and knew the man with the Henry was weighing up the odds. Then, finding them wanting, he ruefully shook his head.

'Well, well,' he said. 'What I should have done is pulled the trigger soon as I saw you. Rode back into town. Collected the cash money.'

'In case you're interested,' Bywater said, 'the man behind you has a sawn-off American Arms 12-gauge pointing at your back.'

There was an oily metallic click as Texas Jack cocked the double-barrelled weapon.

'And if you don't let that pre-war rifle fall into the mud,' the old-timer said, 'you'll be lookin' at your innards splattered all over the man settin' on that fine black mare, the man you came here to kill — '

The flat report of a rifle cut into Texas Jack Logan's words. In the same instant the shotgun was plucked from his hands. It flew high, its butt splintered, and splashed into the North Platte.

Loomis had one good eye, but two sharp ears. He heard the bullet's impact, followed by the splash. Instinct told him what had happened. That same instinct should have told him to fire the Henry from the hip and down Bywater before turning to face the other man. Instead, he held his fire and used a knee to spin his horse so that he could see both Bywater and Texas Jack, who was cursing loudly in between sucking his bruised fingers.

Then, as lightning flashed, searing the eyes, Loomis finally began lifting the Henry rifle.

He was too late.

Action had turned time on its head. Bywater seemed to watch for an age as the Henry's barrel come up; seemed to have all the time in the world to reach a decision on how he should react. When he did make that decision and explode into action, it was as if his Colt .45 leaped from its holster. The butt smacked into his palm. His finger held the trigger back. His left hand whipped across his body, fanned the hammer twice. With the pistol's sear disengaged, the hammer was free to drop. Two shots rang out in rapid succession. Floyd Loomis rocked in the saddle, clutching his shoulder. His horse reared, hoofs cutting the air.

Loomis toppled backwards out of the saddle. His head hit the ground hard. He groaned, and lay still.

Since the crack of the first shot, mere split seconds had passed. Bywater's two shots were sandwiched between the rifle shot that shattered Texas Jack's shotgun butt and a second shot that almost took off Bywater's right ear. He ducked sideways as the hot lead hummed by, cast a glance north up the inland trail and saw Hank Geary and Parker Laing spurring their horses down towards the river. Laing was the man with the rifle. He was waving it aloft, and screaming. There was no sign of Nathan Wedge.

'Jack,' Bywater yelled, 'you got a weapon?'

The old-timer slapped a hand to his side. It came up holding his huge .44 Dragoon Colt.

'Get down to the river, into the trees.'

Suddenly rain lashed out of the east in hissing, sweeping sheets, cutting visibility to a few hundred yards. Out of that opaque veil of water the two gunmen came racing as Bywater spurred Doone down to the cottonwoods and leaped from the saddle.

Texas Jack Logan was already in the trees, his sandy beard glistening as he aimed the Dragoon at the approaching riders. Again thunder rumbled. Then the Dragoon roared. The huge muzzle flash lit up the trees. As if in retaliation, the expected lightning bolt hissed from the sky and struck the ground a hundred yards away with a blinding white flash.

The flash died. Sight returned. And glancing upstream, Bywater saw Clarence Sugg urging his pony along the riverbank.

Suddenly he was aware of Texas Jack's six-gun blasting away. As he dashed the rain from his eyes the big gun went silent. He saw the old-timer dig into his pocket, come up with a handful of brass shells and begin calmly to reload: in the interests of speed, the heavy old revolver had been converted from percussion.

A hasty glance beyond Texas Jack told Bywater that Geary and Laing were racing down the slope and would be upon them in seconds. He whipped out his Colt and began blasting away as hoofs thundered behind him. Then Clarence Sugg was down out of the saddle and, from the next tree, shots began pounding like the deep measured beat of a bass drum.

Already the carefully aimed fire from three men in excellent cover was paying off. Geary and Laing had been caught out in the open. Geary's horse was down. But both gunmen had flattened themselves in the short grass, and were blasting wild shots through the rain.

Then Sugg spoke up. 'In this weather, anything could go wrong,' he cried. 'I say we back off, live to fight another day. There's three of us. Enough for good covering fire and an orderly retreat.'

When Bywater looked across, the lean Pinkerton man was grinning and gesturing towards the cabin.

Christ, it's not the chance of one of those two getting in a lucky shot that's bothering him, Bywater marvelled, it's the rain.

'Jack,' he called, still shaking his head, 'start moving back to your cabin. Pass behind me. I'll cover you. Bony, you go with him.'

As Texas Jack pouched his weapon and came by at a crouching run, Bywater punched shells into his Colt and began firing in the direction of the prone gunmen. He spaced his shots, calculating one for each ten yards his companions could run. He reached the sixth, fired the final shot — and heard Clarence Sugg's sing-song halloo. At once, the two heavy pistols opened up from sixty yards away.

Temple Bywater climbed to his feet and ran.

His ears were filled with the conflicting sounds of his own pounding footsteps, his rasping breath, the hiss of rain, the rumble of thunder. He could see muzzle flashes, and hear the crack of Sugg's and Logan's pistols — but from behind him he could hear nothing.

'They're up and running,' Texas Jack said as Bywater reached them, and his eyes glittered with contempt as he gazed back the way they had come and spat in the grass.

'So are we,' Sugg pointed out. 'And it's still half a mile to the cabin.'

'Yeah, but with both factions heading in opposite directions,' Bywater said, 'I'd say the fight's over.'

'Over before it started,' Texas Jack said. 'Come on, let's get inside and dry off — and you can tell us what the hell that was all about.'

★   ★   ★

That telling took the three men long past the midnight hour. It started as an intelligent discussion on the current investigation, but descended into sometimes merry and often maudlin reminiscing on past Pinkerton investigations.

In particular they recalled a case, some fifteen years ago, that had taken them all the way east to New York in pursuit of a businessman who had made a fortune by fleecing Texas ranchers in the days of the cattle drives up the Chisholm trail. When they embarked on what came to be known as the East Side Travesty, Texas Jack was a Pinkerton veteran, Bywater and Sugg rookies on their first important case. Getting past the white-collar criminal's crooked lawyer and hunting him down had presented no problems; when they cornered him in a shabby apartment block he had enlisted the services of half-a-dozen city villains and, in a bloody showdown, Temple Bywater had been shot through the upper arm and would have died had it not been for Texas Jack's raw courage.

The man was a Pinkerton legend. Memories of his exploits had lingered with Bywater long after the man had departed, and recollections of that one story were enough to drastically lower the level of moonshine whiskey in Texas Jack Logan's big jug. The inevitable result was that, next morning, Temple Bywater rolled out of his blankets on the cabin floor with the conviction that his head was being painfully split in two, from the inside.

7

The sun was bouncing off the street's dust as a searing white glare when Temple Bywater and Clarence Sugg rode into Saratoga. They'd followed the North Platte from Texas Jack Logan's riverside cabin, noting as they rode out through the hanging river mist the scattering of empty shell cases like glittering yellow beetles in the wet grass; the dead body of Hank Geary's horse glistening on the sloping bank; the absence of Floyd 'Grave' Loomis — dead or alive.

When they reached the town's outskirts, time, for Temple Bywater, had slipped back twenty-four hours.

Just as he had done the previous morning, they rode into Saratoga with Medicine Bow Peak at their backs. The same swamper was hard at work with his pail of water outside Ike Adams's saloon; horses and wagons were again hitched both sides of the street; the sidewalks were alive with people, and shops and commercial premises were open for business. The ring of hammer on anvil was again music to the ears, but there was no ragged youngster sprinting down the plankwalk to warn the town marshal that a stranger was bringing in the dead body of the town mayor's son.

The young boy wasn't needed. As if sensing their approach, Marshal Tom Gaines and his son were outside the jail watching their progress down the street. And when Temple Bywater stepped down from his horse, he was again met by a drawn six-gun.

This time it was held by Deputy Arch Gaines. Marshal Tom Gaines was doing the talking.

'You're under arrest,' he said. 'Both of you. Hand over your gunbelts, then step inside the jail.'

'What's the charge?' Bywater said.

'Murder.'

The sun beat down. Passers by had stopped to watch, some seeking shade, some fanning themselves with their hats. There was an excited buzz of talk.

Bywater exchanged glances with Sugg, then shook his head almost imperceptibly and unbuckled his gun-belt. He handed it to Tom Gaines, waited for Sugg to do the same, then walked ahead of him into the jail.

With the door closed, Arch Gaines pouched his weapon and moved to the window so that he was behind the arrested men. Tom Gaines sat behind his desk, skimmed his Stetson neatly onto a wooden peg and rocked back in his swivel chair.

'Got anything to say for yourselves?'

'Who, where, and when?' Bywater said.

He was standing alongside Sugg, in front of the desk. Two schoolkids, he thought, mildly amused. Up in front of the headmaster.

'Floyd Loomis. Late yesterday afternoon. He was shot dead close to Texas

Jack Logan's cabin. Two slugs in the shoulder, one through the heart.'

Bywater shook his head. 'That's not right.'

'You saying you had nothing to do with the shooting?'

'I'm admitting I planted the slugs in his shoulder. But not the one that killed him.' He thought for a moment. 'Where's the body?'

'Down at Joe Ringling's.'

'Check the wounds. I use a .45, so does Sugg. That's unusual — '

Gaines shook his head. 'Not necessary. Two witnesses saw him gunned down.'

Alongside Bywater, Clarence Sugg said something that sounded like, 'Ho hum,' and yawned prodigiously.

'I suppose that must be Geary and Laing,' Bywater said, fighting an involuntary smile. 'Two men who served time in the pen with Gus Allman. Problem is, ex-cons don't make reliable witnesses.'

'They're frightened men. They'll

testify that they were attacked by you, your sidekick here, and Texas Jack Logan. Before that, they saw Loomis blasted out of his saddle.'

'Did they also tell you they saw Loomis throw down on me with an old Henry rifle?'

'It was in the middle of a violent summer storm. They saw the muzzle flashes, saw Loomis go down. In the ensuing gun battle, Hank Geary lost a fine horse and both men consider themselves lucky to be alive. Late last night they brought Loomis in, belly down, Geary and Laing riding double on Laing's horse.'

'Are you prepared to take their word over the word of two Pinkerton operatives? Three, if you count Texas Jack: he worked out of the Denver office until he retired ten years ago.'

Gaines rocked thoughtfully, lips pursed. He looked across at his son; back at Bywater.

'I didn't know that. He spends most of his time downriver, comes in maybe once a month for supplies.' He flapped a hand dismissively. 'But it changes nothing. I've got a man dead of gunshot wounds, and two witnesses. You're saying those witnesses are lying. Fine, get yourself a good lawyer and they'll be exposed in court. Until then — '

'Jesus Christ,' Clarence Sugg said softly. 'You're going to lock us up when we're in Saratoga investigating the death of your newly elected senator? Hasn't it occurred to you that you're playing into the hands of ruthless men who are hell bent on buying time?'

Gaines frowned. 'For what?'

'Someone's about to step into Andrew Stone's shoes. When does that happen?'

'A day . . . two at the outside.'

'If you lock us up for *any* length of time, the men buying that time are home and dry.'

'Maybe that suits the marshal,' Bywater said carefully. 'He and Forrest Jackson lied through their teeth over Gus Allman's acquaintances. Now we know Jackson's brother's in line for the senatorship, that behaviour begins to look mighty suspicious — '

The swivel chair rolled back so fast it crashed into the wall as Tom Gaines lurched to his feet. His eyes were blazing.

'Enough,' he said tightly. 'You know the charge — '

'Yes, but why drag Sugg into it?'

'He's an accessory to murder. So is Texas Jack Logan, and he'll be picked up.' Gaines waited, got no reaction and went on, 'Now, if you want a lawyer — '

'Get me Forrest Jackson,' Bywater said.

Gaines shrugged. 'Your choice. I'll see if he's in town, ask him if he's free to discuss the charges with you. In the meantime . . . Deputy Gaines, take the prisoners out back, and lock them up — in separate cells.'

★　★　★

'If Geary and Laing murdered Grave Loomis and are trying to pin it on you,' Clarence Sugg said, 'who's paying

96

them? Wedge, or the Fort Steele lawyer, Millard Jackson?'

'When they followed me they were riding with Nathan Wedge. But it was Loomis who tried to kill me. If Wedge was paying Geary and Laing, who was paying Loomis?'

'According to Wedge,' Sugg said, 'he was paying those two ex-cons for one day's work: they were bodyguards for his ride upriver after you.'

'Which means that at all other times they could have been Millard Jackson's hired killers. If so, then, without realizing it, Wedge was putting himself in danger by hiring them.' He paused. 'If the two excons were Jackson's boys, then Loomis was acting for Wedge. And with the backing of a big-time politician, Wedge will have more clout than a small town lawyer like Millard Jackson.'

'Maybe, but if we're right, Geary and Laing took out his hired killer. Looks to me like they seized the opportunity to get rid of him when you knocked him off his horse.'

The cells Arch Gaines had locked them in were opposite each other. Between the cells there was an open space with a table set on a dirt floor, a couple of straight chairs, an oil lamp. Striped sunlight was slanting through high barred windows and falling across the table. In the uncomfortably hot cells, both men were lying back on thin corn-husk mattresses, their faces filmed with sweat. Bywater was idly watching the thin ribbon of smoke rising from the cigarette smouldering between his fingers. Sugg had his hands clasped behind his head.

'Of course,' Bywater said, 'we could be talking a load of bull. We're taking it for granted Stone was killed because he got to be senator, then jumping to the conclusion that the man behind his murder must be Wedge or Jackson. But what if there was a skeleton in Stone's past, and this was a revenge killing? Or maybe his wife was seeing someone when he was out chasing votes, and killing him seemed to this fellow like a good way of getting at Stone's fortune.'

'Somehow those last two options seem more plausible than a couple of aspiring politicians resorting to bloodshed,' Clarence Sugg said. 'But if we go down that road we open up a whole range of possibilities limited only by a good Pinkerton man's imagination — and while we're locked up in here there's not a damn thing we can do about it.'

Bywater looked at the glowing end of his cigarette.

'Those possibilities should include the town mayor, Homer Allman — a man I've been overlooking — '

'And he's left town?'

'Yes. But remember it was his son, Gus, who came after me. Allman was ambitious enough to get elected mayor, so why stop there? Maybe he'll return, and we'll see another hat thrown in the ring, another man offer himself up as a suspect . . . '

There was a lengthy silence as both men cogitated.

'Tom Gaines bothers me,' Bywater said at last. 'He's the man charging us with murder and, now I think back, it was Gaines who lied about Allman.'

'The man who shot you when you rode down from the hills?'

'Right. When I was in Forrest Jackson's office it was Gaines, not Jackson, who asserted Allman did not mix with men of standing; Gaines who said the only time he saw Allman talking to a man of authority was when he cursed the judge who sentenced him.'

Sugg frowned. 'That suggests Gaines is hiding something. But what? Did he have Stone killed? Did Gaines — ?'

He broke off as Bywater jerked upright, shot a glance towards the opening into the office and flapped an urgent warning hand. Seconds later Tom Gaines walked through, followed by Forrest Jackson and a man so like him it had to be his younger brother.

★   ★   ★

Marshal Tom Gaines was once again behind his desk, but the look on his face had changed from guarded triumph to one of barely suppressed anger.

He had brought the rickety wooden chairs through from the cell area, and Bywater and Sugg were sitting on those. Forrest Jackson and his brother, Millard, occupied the office's other chairs.

Both Bywater and Sugg were wearing their gunbelts.

'Arch Gaines told me the story concocted by Geary and Laing,' Forrest Jackson said for Bywater's benefit. 'Utter nonsense. My brother was with me in my office when Arch brought the news. We immediately walked across the street to talk to Doc Benson, took him with us down to Joe Ringling's and got him to cut open that man Loomis. Benson pulled out all three slugs. The one that killed Loomis was noticeably smaller than the other two — I'd say a .44.'

'Geary carries a Remington Frontier .44,' Millard Jackson chipped in.

Bywater glared at the marshal.

'Have you pulled him in?'

'He left town. Him and his sidekick.'

'But when you find him, he'll be charged — and those against us have been dropped?'

Gaines scowled. 'You're free to go, both of you. But that doesn't mean I like it. Two of your slugs knocked that man off his horse. He could have been dead from those before Geary drilled him through the heart.'

'Conjecture,' Forrest Jackson said disdainfully. 'Not admissible in any court of law.'

'Jesus Christ,' Tom Gaines growled, climbing out of his seat, 'will you all get the hell out of here and let me get on with my day!'

8

'What do we do now?'

The door had slammed shut behind Bywater and Sugg. The office was less crowded, but the air crackled with tension. Millard Jackson lit a cigar. Tom Gaines turned his back and poured a cup of coffee for himself. Neither man answered Forrest Jackson's question.

'A bigger worry for all of us,' Marshal Gaines said as he swung round to face them, 'is what *they* are going to do.'

'Oh, Bywater will busy himself investigating a murder,' Forrest said placidly.

'A man looking for treasure doesn't need to dig very deep,' Millard Jackson said, 'before he finds a mess of worms.'

'Depends where he plants his spade,' Forrest said, 'and I'd say we're safe. Bywater's sure to begin with the young widow. All she knows is she became a rich woman overnight.'

'Same when, or if, he gets to Homer Allman,' Millard said around his fat cigar. 'A windbag. If our illustrious mayor does return to Saratoga and talk, he'll spout hot air, leaving Bywater with nothing.'

Forrest Jackson chuckled softly.

Gaines glared. 'What the hell's so funny?'

'My brother tells us Bywater will know nothing. But aren't we in the same boat? I certainly am. Oh, I know what you've done, Millard, and you, Tom. But that knowledge is limited to what you want me to know — or what you cannot prevent me from knowing. What I do not know is if either of you had anything to do with the death of Andrew Stone.'

Millard took the cigar from his mouth. The end was moist. His eyes were unreadable as he faced his elder brother.

'Same goes for me. You're a man with a lot of secrets, Forrest. So let's just say there are some things none of us needs to know. And you for one should be well content: with Gus Allman dead, you're saving money each and every month.'

'Oh yes,' Forrest said, 'those payments were an irritating inconvenience. But their welcome absence leads to another imponderable: who hired young Gus Allman, sent him out there to get killed?'

'Let's stick with your first question: what do we do now?'

'It was rhetorical: I already have the answer.'

'Which is?'

'We do nothing. Bywater will talk to the grieving widow. Eventually, he will get to us. When that happens, I'll ask the same question.'

'Yeah,' Tom Gaines said, his face bleak. 'And if he gets that close and we want to stay out of jail, there's only the one answer.'

9

Tom Gaines's parting shot accurately reflected Temple Bywater's mood. After being in Saratoga for a little more than twenty-four hours he had accomplished nothing, and was desperate to move on.

Immediately on walking out of the jail, he and Sugg picked up their mounts from Cole's livery barn where they had been taken by Deputy Arch Gaines, and led them across the street to the saloon. Ike Adams was behind the bar, grinning broadly. After Bywater had dealt with the introductions, the saloonist told them he'd heard about their troubles and hadn't believed a word of the murder accusation. As a token of his goodwill and to celebrate their release, he presented both men with cool beers, compliments of the house. Then, clearly intrigued by the unfolding drama, he willingly gave Bywater directions to the house where Andrew Stone's widow, Elizabeth, was living with her grief.

It was, Adams said, a fine white mansion standing ten miles north of Saratoga, at the fork where Sage Creek joined the North Platte. On the river's west bank and roughly halfway between Saratoga and Fort Steele — where the North Platte and the Union Pacific Railway crossed — the location, for Bywater's purposes, was ideal.

'I'll go on from the Stone place to Fort Steele,' he said as he and Sugg rode out of town, their horses' hoofs drumming on the worn boards of the timber bridge over the river. 'From there I'll wire Denver, then finish the day seeing if I can dig up anything useful on Millard Jackson.'

'With nothing to report to Eames, isn't the Denver wire a waste of time?'

'I want information. Anything Charlie can dig up on Stone, Jackson, Wedge — and Bradley Wynne, the rich man backing Nathan Wedge.'

'And where am I while all this is going on?'

Bywater cast his partner a glance. 'Most of the time, you're invisible. I want you to shadow me, at a distance. Geary and Laing left town, but they won't be far away. Look on the killing of Floyd Loomis as a step too far. The aim was to get you and me locked up. That didn't work, but those two ex-cons have shown their hand. For them, and the man who's paying them, there's no going back.'

'We thought that was Millard Jackson. Doesn't look that way now, does it?'

'No, but it doesn't make them any less dangerous.'

'You reckon they're out there now, watching us?'

'You can bet your whiskers on it,' Bywater said.

★　★　★

Timber white enough to make a man flinch when sunlight hit the walls, a portico supported by six columns stretching the full width of the house, a backdrop of dark pines specially planted, and a gleaming top-buggy in front of the house on the wide drive covered in stone chippings that curved up from the trail through sweeping lawns showing clear signs of neglect.

As Bywater rode up to the Stone house he could see everything he had expected except for signs of life. But this, he reminded himself, was the house built by a man who had made his fortune fully thirty years ago in the Pike's Peak gold-rush, and later moved north to Saratoga to find peace. His money had helped establish the town's hot springs. He had busied himself in marketing and development. But the ten miles he had put between his business and his home was a testimony to his desire for restful solitude, a barrier against unwanted intrusion. As far as Bywater knew, that barrier had been effective until Stone became restless, successfully stood for State

Senator and was looking forward to a late-life career until a man rode in and shot him in the back.

He hitched Doone to a peeled rail that even this opulent residence could not do without, then walked into the shade of the portico and rapped on the door. It was answered remarkably quickly. He guessed that his approach had been observed from the moment he left the river.

The woman was tall and slim. Her thick hair was snatched back in a golden skein. The eyes he had expected to be pools of sadness looked at him questioningly, and her long dress was not made for mourning.

Bywater smiled, and doffed his hat. 'Mrs Stone?'

She nodded.

'My name is Temple Bywater. I work for the Pinkertons. I wonder — '

She silenced him with a raised hand and a half smile.

'I've heard about you, Mr Bywater. Do come in.'

She led him into a living room overlooking the front of the house, waved him to a seat and watched him sink into it gingerly and place his hat on the cushions.

'Is it too early for a glass of wine?'

About ten years, Bywater thought, at the rate I make money. Burying the notion, he shook his head.

'I'll give it a miss. If you don't mind I'd like to get on, ask you a few questions.'

'In a moment.'

She crossed the room to a cabinet, selected a glass, picked up an open bottle. While she was occupied, Bywater looked around, admiring the room. He saw large windows, expensive furniture, walls where oil paintings hung — there was a space that might once have been filled by a small one — and an elaborate crystal chandelier hanging over a polished table set on animal skin rugs.

The smell of money. This was a poor girl who had become rich in the time it took for a trigger to be pulled, a bullet to strike soft flesh. Listening in his mind to her softly spoken words, Bywater again recalled the Pinkertons' involvement in the East Side Travesty, the people he had met, and he knew that this woman was from the east coast, probably New York. And he wondered if that degree of big-city sophistication, bred into her, made her more or less likely to take the law into her own hands if the need, or desire, arose.

Glass clinked, bringing him back down to earth. Elizabeth Stone carried her glass to a chair and sat down opposite him, her free hand curled primly in her lap.

'I saw you looking at that blank space on the wall, Mr Bywater. It's ugly, isn't it?'

'Not of itself. But if you mean because of the absence of something beautiful . . . '

She bobbed her head in acknowledgement of a simple truth.

'The missing item was not beautiful, but it was treasured. A plaque used to hang there. It reminded my husband of earlier times, and so it was something he loved to look at.' She smiled sadly. 'The man who murdered him broke into this room, and stole it.'

Bywater murmured suitable words of sympathy, and again she bobbed her head. As she did so, a horse whinnied, far off, and was answered immediately by Doone. That's Clarence Sugg's paint, Bywater thought. But why is Sugg coming this way? With a plan agreed to, he would only change it if there was trouble.

He frowned, saw Elizabeth Stone watching him, and got down to business.

'You know why the Pinkertons have been called in,' Bywater began. 'Your husband had been elected as Wyoming's second senator, and then he was murdered. It's highly likely his election and death were linked. If that's true, then there are obvious suspects. But, apart from those men whose names

I'm sure you know, did your husband have any enemies?'

'I know of none.'

'Were you at home on the day he died?'

'I was in Forte Steele. I took the buggy there in the early morning and stayed all day.'

'Alone?'

'No.'

'Can I ask who you were with?'

'No.'

'Were you with Nathan Wedge?'

'Your question is impertinent. I certainly won't answer.'

'You understand the conclusion that leads to?'

'Certainly. But as I won't comment, you must make up your own mind.'

Bywater sighed in frustration. Elizabeth Stone's lips twitched. She said nothing.

'Have you any thoughts on who murdered your husband?'

'Possibly. They probably match yours. But it really doesn't matter. Andrew is dead and, one way or another, I will soon be somewhere far away.'

'You're selling up, moving on?'

She dipped her head in affirmation; glanced quickly towards the window at the sound of horse's hoofs approaching, Doone's soft snort of welcome.

Sugg, Bywater thought. He's very close. He lifted an eyebrow as Elizabeth turned her gaze his way, and decided to try shock tactics.

'Expecting somebody, Mrs Stone? Perhaps this Fort Steele . . . acquaintance?'

She shook her head.

'And what about the move? Are you leaving because of your husband's death?'

'No.'

'Is this move linked to the man you were with in Forte Steele?'

'Why do you presume it was a man?'

'Was it?'

She took a sip of wine, gazed at him over the rim of the glass. They both heard the horse draw closer. The sudden silence as it drew to a halt.

'The questions you ask, and the way you ask them,' Elizabeth Stone said, 'suggest I'm one of your suspects. Do you believe I had something to do with my husband's death?'

'In cases of murder, suspicion always falls on surviving family members,' Bywater said, 'especially those coming into a great deal of money.'

'What if I told you I have no need of his money? That I would be quite comfortably provided for had Andrew lived, or died?'

'Provided for?' Bywater said. 'Well now, the way you put that makes me even more suspicious — and there's nothing more dangerous than a Pinkerton man who gets a whiff of guilt.'

She smiled mysteriously and, with a sudden soft exclamation, Bywater rose to his feet.

'Aren't you curious about the new arrival?'

'Not in the least.'

He grunted, left her clutching her wine glass and strode out of the room to the front door. When he dragged it open, he was met by a blast of warm air and the faint beginnings of a smell he recognized. His skin prickled. He stepped out of the house, walked out from under the portico's shade into hot sunlight and saw a riderless horse standing with drooping head, foam-flecked withers. Its chest was heaving, nostrils flaring.

It was Clarence Sugg's paint pony — but Sugg was nowhere to be seen. The paint's reins were trailing, effectively tethering the quivering animal. As Bywater moved closer, uttering soft, soothing words, his own nostrils flared at the familiar coppery odour now being intensified by the hot sun. He reached out a hand, traced with his fingertips the fancy leather tooling of the Pinkerton man's California saddle; then grimaced as he touched the sticky blood that was staining the fork, the seat, the cantle, and had run in dark, ugly rivulets across the Winchester in its boot under the left fender.

10

Temple Bywater found Sugg by the North Platte. The lanky Pinkerton man was sitting on the bank close to the water. His elbows were on his knees, his head in his hands. The hair on the side of his head was matted with blood, the back of his shirt soaked through and stiffening, his fingers caked.

His thoughts must have been miles away. He remained still as Bywater, leading the paint pony on a short rope, approached on Doone. Then dry brush crackled under the horses' hoofs. Sugg suddenly realized he could be in danger. With an audible curse he rolled sideways on the grass, a hand stabbing for his pistol.

When he caught sight of Bywater, he groaned, flopped backwards and folded a forearm over his eyes.

'Don't ask me,' he said, still covering

his eyes as Bywater dismounted. 'I'm shadowing you like a goddamn Indian, next thing I know is I'm coming to, flat on my back with my feet in the river. My horse has gone, seems like someone I can't see is banging my head with a blacksmith's hammer, and I'm losing pints of good blood.'

'Scalp wounds are like that,' Bywater said, hunkering down by him and proffering a canteen. 'Bleeding stops as quick as it starts.' He leaned close, looking without touching. 'A bullet grazed your scalp, Bony. We slipped up: while you were watching me, Geary and Laing were watching you.'

Sugg sat up, wincing, and drank from the canteen. He jerked his head towards the paint, and winced again as the sudden movement squeezed his eyes shut.

'Where did you find her?'

'She found Doone. I was in the Stone house.'

'Worth the visit?'

'I'm not sure. I know more now than

119

I did, but I'll be damned if I know what it means.'

'Tell me about it on the way to Fort Steele.' Sugg squinted at him. 'I take it that's where we're going?'

'If you're fit enough.'

'Hell, it's just a scratch,' Sugg said. He stood up quickly, staggered sideways, tripped over his own feet and finished up flat on his back.

For one concerned moment Bywater thought the sound he could hear was the wounded Pinkerton man choking. Then he turned away, shaking his head. Clarence Sugg, eyes streaming, face red, was helpless with laughter.

★   ★   ★

Dusk was deepening into night when they rode into Fort Steele and, when they'd hitched their horses outside the saloon, Bywater's first call was to the telegraph office. There he scribbled a message on one of the regulation forms, and sent his wire to Charlie Eames in the Pinkerton's Denver office.

On his way back up the street from the railroad he found Clarence Sugg washing dried blood off his face and hands under the pump outside the livery barn. Sugg followed that by stripping off his shirt, drying his face with the stiff cloth then washing the shirt in the trough and wringing it almost dry. Shivering, he slipped on the cold, damp garment.

'Right,' he said, turning to Bywater, 'let's go talk to Millard Jackson.'

'What about a doctor? That wound needs attention.'

Sugg reached to his head, probed gingerly.

'It's scabbing over. Interfering with it now will draw more blood — and I'm plumb empty.' He grinned. 'Right, Jackson?'

'His office is over there,' Bywater said, pointing across the street. 'Closed for the day. But we don't want to talk to him, we need to talk to people who know him. So look around. Where do you see lights?'

Sugg turned slowly, surveying the scene.

'Hotel. Café. The saloon, and the jail.'

'Take your pick.'

'I'm thirsty.'

'I passed the jail on the way up the street. I swear I smelled fresh coffee.'

Despite Sugg's voluble protests, it proved to be the right decision. Marshal Ronan Kerrigan did indeed have java bubbling on his office stove, and when the red-headed Irish lawman had scrutinized the Pinkerton men's official badges he was happy to fill three cups with the hot black brew, sit back in his chair and listen to their story.

Sugg had been brought up to date on the ride in to Fort Steele. Kerrigan got an abridged version, which didn't take long to tell.

'I heard about Stone's death,' he said, when Bywater had finished. 'Mill Jackson entering the race to take his place is news to me.' His blue eyes narrowed as he tugged at his ragged dragoon moustache. 'And now you want my assessment of — of what, exactly?'

'Background and character,' Bywater said helpfully. 'Is Jackson hiding anything? If so, what?'

'Mill Jackson's a lawyer,' Kerrigan said, with a crooked grin. 'That answers your first question.'

'And the second?'

'He hung out his shingle here in Fort Steele maybe fifteen years ago. Stepped off the train carrying a leather briefcase, opened his office, got down to business. Most of his duties since have been humdrum. Wills, probate, sorting out land disputes, water rights. Once in a while he's done some genuine courtroom work, won more times than he lost.'

'Gus Allman was one he lost.'

'Right. Gus was tried here, in the hotel.'

'Cut and dried?'

'By no means.' Kerrigan shrugged. 'A lot of folk thought Gus Allman was innocent, including me. But Tom Gaines from Saratoga arrested him, and when it came to the decision the jury found Allman guilty and he was sent to the pen. You could say Mill Jackson ended up with egg on his face.'

'Was that a first for him?'

'Here it was. He usually comes out on top. But rumour has it he suffered a lot worse back East.'

The bells that had first started ringing in Ike Adams's saloon in Saratoga again began jangling furiously, and Bywater felt his pulse quicken.

Clarence Sugg was watching him with a half smile.

'You thinking what I'm thinking? A lawyer, working on the east coast?'

'Damn right I am.' He looked at Kerrigan. 'You said he set up office fifteen years ago?'

'Almost to the day.'

'And he came in by rail. From where, do you know?'

'Someone I spoke to knew him in New York. Jackson was a big-time lawyer. But something went so badly wrong, moving West was his only option.'

'Was the East Side Travesty mentioned?'

'What the hell's that?'

'If I'm getting the right answer when I add two and two, Jackson was in the pay of New York crooks. He almost went down with them in an operation involving the Pinkertons and the New York Police. It was a mess, hence the name.'

'You saying you were there?'

'Both of us were.' Bywater nodded at Sugg. 'Rookies, under the wing of a seasoned detective called Texas Jack Logan.'

Kerrigan was shaking his head. 'You've got more information than me. You sure you need my help?'

Bywater hesitated, looked hopefully at Sugg.

'The answer to your wire,' Sugg suggested. 'Wouldn't it be safest if Kerrigan here collects that, holds it for you.'

'Hell, yes.' Bywater quickly explained,

and Kerrigan readily agreed.

'I'm out of here,' he said then, climbing out of his chair. 'I take a walk around about this time every evening, keep the old folks happy and the youngsters from shooting up the town. If you're planning on booking in at the hotel, why don't you walk up with me?'

Bywater shook his head as he and Sugg made for the door.

'The moon's up,' he said. 'We head back to Saratoga now it should be a pleasant night ride along the river.'

★   ★   ★

'You were talking about putting two and two together back in Kerrigan's office,' Sugg said, 'and I've been doing some addition of my own. The answer I arrived at could be bad for Nathan Wedge.'

'You mean his career prospects could nosedive.'

Sugg chuckled. 'Yeah. If he wanted to do what I think he's doing, he should've waited until he got himself elected.'

The moonlight was filtering through the grey-green cottonwoods, the North Platte was a flat ribbon of silver, and the two Pinkerton men were riding in a leisurely way along banks already glistening with dew. They were approaching the point where Sage Creek joined the bigger river. As this was getting close to the Stone residence, Bywater guessed the proximity had nudged his sidekick's thoughts in that direction.

'According to Forrest Jackson, Hedge has been assisting at the Fort Steele bank twice every month,' Bywater said. 'That ride takes him mighty close to Elizabeth Stone.'

'If he's been assisting for a year, he was passing the house when Stone was alive,' Sugg pointed out. 'Stone's business interests were with the hot springs in Saratoga. If Hedge timed it right he could start out for the Fort Steele bank and tip his hat to Stone, just about here, as they passed on the trail.'

'Could be wild conjecture,' Bywater

said, 'but if there was an assignation it would explain Elizabeth Stone's saying she was comfortably provided for, with or without her rich husband.'

Bridles jingled, and the soft breeze rustled the leaves as Bywater and Sugg rode alongside the river in silence, ruminating on the possibility of an ambitious man's infidelity.

Bywater was also reflecting on how a straightforward murder investigation had branched out in several directions to give them a number of possible motives — not for the original murder of Andrew Stone, but for subsequent attacks on the two Pinkerton men.

The easy assumption was that the attacks were to prevent the Pinkerton men from tracking down Stone's killer. That might still be true. But Mill Jackson was a crooked lawyer from way back, and it was possible Nathan Hedge — a married man — had been philandering. If either man had killed to open the way to national government, a successful bid for the senatorship now depended on their keeping those indiscretions secret.

And there was another unanswered question. Why had Gus Allman been visiting Forrest Jackson ever since he got out of the state pen? The link was his unsuccessful defence by Mill Jackson, Forrest's once crooked brother. But that link became blurred when Marshal Tom Gaines was brought in, because he too had lied when questioned about Gus Allman . . .

'I hate to take the shine off a beautiful evening,' Clemence Sugg said, breaking into his thoughts, 'but there's two riders up ahead of us. Far as I can make out, one's Hank Geary. The other I don't recognize.'

'No, neither do I,' Temple Bywater said as the menacing sound of a shell being slammed home in a rifle's breech broke the stillness of the night. 'But I reckon the itchy-fingered man with the rifle is Parker Laing — and he's right behind us.'

11

'Draw your six-guns nice and easy with finger and thumb, then see if you can toss them into the river,' Hank Geary said.

The rawboned gunman was sneering, moonlight shining on his ragged blond hair. His horse was turned side-on. He held a Winchester across his body. It stayed trained on the Pinkerton men as they carried out his orders. Sugg reached the river with his throw, and was rewarded with a splash. Bywater's six-gun hit a tree.

'Want me to get down,' he said, 'and try again?'

The big man sitting a little way behind Geary on a well-groomed sorrel showed white teeth in a smile. Comfortably padded, Bywater noticed, and guessed the soft bulk had been acquired through years of good eating. The cash that had bought him fine food had extended to expensive clothing. The smell of money was oozing from every bathed and perfumed pore, and one name at once sprang to Bywater's mind: Bradley Wynne, the rich man backing Nathan Wedge.

As Geary relaxed and lowered his rifle, Parker Laing showed himself. He came from behind, riding a powerful blood bay around the Pinkerton men then backing the horse into the trees. The weapon whose action they'd heard being worked was a single-shot Sharps buffalo gun. It never wavered. The look on the man's swarthy face told Bywater that he'd like nothing better than for one of them to make a wrong move.

Now the big man took over. He touched the sorrel with the heels of his gleaming boots and rode between the two gunmen. Ten feet from the Pinkerton men, he stopped.

'I've come with a proposal,' he said. 'One I'm quite sure you will accept.'

'Sounds confident,' Sugg said, looking at Bywater.

'Or conceited,' Bywater suggested.

'And either way, he's wrong.'

'Shut up,' Parker Laing said, 'and listen.'

A soft leather pouch appeared in the big man's hand. He hefted it, let them see the weight.

'This is gold dust,' he said. 'I'll leave its worth to your imagination.' He paused, waited until he considered they'd done enough imagining, then said, 'It's yours to share, no strings, if you keep riding and don't stop until you reach Denver.'

'Isn't that a string?' Bywater said.

'I prefer to call it a condition.'

'And what do we tell our boss, Charlie Eames?'

'That you believe the man who shot down Andrew Stone has left Wyoming. Gone, you know not where; to go after him would be a waste of time and effort.' The big man shrugged. 'Or make up your own story.'

'We'd have to,' Clarence Sugg said, 'because the man who shot Stone's still around.'

'One small lie,' the big man says, 'will make you both very rich.'

'But allow a killer to go free,' Bywater said softly.

'It's irrelevant. I want an answer. Yes or no?'

'I've got my own condition,' Bywater said. 'Or string. Give us Stone's killer, you keep the gold, and we'll ride out.'

'You've got one more minute — and no second chance.'

The liquid murmur of the river was a soporific background to a developing nightmare. Branches rattled overhead like the clicking of dead men's bones. The night air seemed to crackle with the powerful charge that precedes a violent electric storm. Tension mounted unbearably. Bywater waited, his nerves like taut wire.

The man hefting the leather bag of gold dust listened to the night sounds, and said nothing. The answer he required was not forthcoming. His lips tightened. The moonlight picked out furious highlights in his pale-blue eyes.

Sitting with increasing rigidity on the fine sorrel horse, he was a short-tempered man about to explode.

Then it was over.

His sudden indrawn breath, its rapid, frustrated expulsion, were clear signals that time was up. He reached behind and down and dropped the leather pouch into an open saddle-bag, let the flap drop. When he straightened, the tension had left his body and he was once more relaxed and in control.

'Take them across the river,' he said to Parker Laing. 'Lock them up. Keep them until you get word from me. Then kick them out and let them walk home.'

12

The door slammed, cutting off the cold moonlight. Bywater heard a beam fall into place in iron brackets, the crunch of footsteps retreating. As far as he could tell, it was just one man walking back to the big house where lamplight glowed in the windows and a woman watched, white-faced. One man leaving meant one remained: either Hank Geary or Parker Laing was stationed outside the wooden outbuilding. A sentry, guarding the prisoners.

There was a clatter as Clarence Sugg tripped over an unseen object. They were in darkness. The building had no windows. Sugg cursed softly, and Bywater wondered if he'd knocked his head wound, restarted the bleeding. Then there was silence as both men settled down to wait for their eyes to become adjusted to the gloom.

'This is Andrew Stone's woodshed,' Bywater said. 'He was shot dead outside this building while splitting logs for the coming winter.'

'If it's Stone's woodshed,' Sugg said, 'then we're being held here with the permission, or knowledge, of his widow. That suggests our thinking's been on the right lines.'

'On the right lines, but still not proven. If that big man is Bradley Wynne, and if he's backing Nathan Wedge, then it all comes together. Wedge and his wealthy backer are desperate to keep us from the truth, which is that Wedge, a married man and candidate for the senatorship, is having an illicit relationship with Elizabeth Stone — and it was going on when Stone was alive.'

'Two ifs is two too many,' Sugg said.

Bywater's eyes were adjusting. He could see Sugg leaning against a work bench. Crates and barrels, coils of rope, the scent of apples, suggested the woodshed was also used as a store.

sound. Moonlight flooded over his face.

'You'll need a weapon,' Bywater said softly, 'when you come up behind him.'

'That's one thing I learned from you, Temp. Remember that little Remington over-and-under .41?'

'You telling me you've got that popgun tucked away in your boot?'

'You bet,' Sugg said, then ducked his head as another shingle gave way and dust showered down.

'Well, aren't you the crafty so and so,' Bywater said, moving to the door and placing his face close to the boards.

'Hey, Laing,' he called loudly.

There was a sudden shuffling sound.

'That you, Laing?'

'Shut up. Get some sleep.'

'We can't. We're starving, Laing.'

'Laing's in the house.'

'I hope he's taken that Sharps with him.'

A chuckle. 'He didn't. He left it with me.'

Single shot, Bywater thought, with satisfaction. And cumbersome.

'Listen,' he said, 'we don't like the idea of two days locked in here.'

'Tough.'

'So we want to talk to your boss. We're sort of taking a shine to that gold dust.'

He waited, looked back. Sugg had worked his head and shoulders through the jagged hole in the roof. As Bywater watched, he heaved himself up and his long legs disappeared through the opening.

Turning back to the door, Bywater said, 'You hear me?'

'You're wasting your breath, he's not here.'

'Rode out?'

'Saw you two locked up, then headed back to town.'

'Which one of you two's in charge?'

'You know who's in charge, and I told you he rode — '

'Come on, now who's wasting breath? One of you *must* have the authority to deal with us if we accept your man's offer.'

'Yeah, well, nothing was said, but that'd be Parker Laing — '

His words abruptly broke off. An instant's strained silence was followed by a faint, muffled report. A startled grunt. The sound of something heavy and soft dropping to the ground, the drawn-out, wheezing sound of a dying breath being exhaled.

Then the beam scraped in the iron brackets, and the door swung open. As it did so, black clouds drifted across the moon. The house, trees, and the grassland sloping down to the river, were plunged into darkness.

'Stealth was never my strong suit,' Sugg said, carelessly tossing the heavy beam to one side. 'He heard me coming, spun round with that goddamn Sharps — '

'Keep your voice down!'

A still, crumpled form lay on the dew-soaked grass. As Bywater glanced at the downed gunman and stepped quickly out of the woodshed he heard a gruff male voice raised in an anger, a woman's shrill protests. He lifted his gaze. The big white house's front door swung open. Lamplight flooded the drive. A man emerged. He clattered down the steps, walked around the horses dozing at the hitch rail and started towards the woodshed. The yellow light at his back transformed him into a looming, menacing silhouette growing bigger with every stride.

'Back inside,' Bywater hissed.

'What — '

He grabbed Sugg's arm dragged him into the shed.

'Parker Laing's heading this way. Get over there in the corner — '

'You're crazy — '

'No! Geary must be dead. Laing's first thought when he finds him will be we've broken out and run for it.'

'All right, all right — but for Christ's sake shut the door.'

'No. You're not thinking straight. A closed door invites him in. An open door will convince him he's right, that we've hightailed.'

The rapid thud of booted feet on soft ground warned them that the swarthy outlaw was moving with deceptive speed. When Bywater risked a fleeting look outside, he saw that Laing was no more than twenty yards away, and had spotted the body lying on the grass.

'Get down, Bony!'

They slipped silently into the dusty corners on either side of the open door, sank down into impenetrable shadows behind crates packed with orchard fruit. As Bywater crouched with his shoulder hard against the front wall he heard a muttered curse. It was followed by a silence that told him Parker Laing was bending over his fallen colleague.

Then there was the whisper of metal on oiled leather, the sound of a pistol being cocked. The oblong of faint light that marked the door opening faded, suddenly became indistinguishable from the surrounding darkness.

Laing was standing in the doorway.

And in that instant the clouds drifted away from the moon and pale light flooded through the gaping hole in the shingle roof.

Bywater closed his eyes. He thought of Sugg's over-and-under Remington hideaway. One shot had downed Geary. One shot remained. But what was that puny weapon up against? He opened his eyes, squinted around the crate. Laing hadn't picked up the Sharps, but moonlight glinted on the big pistol held out before him as he took another step inside the building. A Colt Peacemaker, the .45 calibre outweighing the Remington's .41 — and with six shots available to Laing . . .

For ten long seconds — a lifetime as the waiting Pinkerton men huddled down and fought to hold their breath — Laing stood inside the woodshed. Then he spat disgustedly, swung around and walked away.

Hastily, Bywater squirmed his way out of the corner and peered after the retreating gunman.

Laing had scooped up the Sharps, and was jogging across the grass. He reached the hitchrail, slid the long gun into the blood bay's saddle boot, then climbed onto the big horse. Within seconds of walking out of the woodshed he was spurring his mount down the slope, and Bywater's last glimpse of him was as he swung along the river-bank and turned the bay towards Saratoga.

13

'We buried Hank Geary in a shallow grave in the cottonwoods,' Bywater said. 'No sense leaving a dead man there for the widow woman to find.'

'Did she see you leave?'

'She was watching from the window. She watched us brought in at gunpoint, watched us ride out free as birds. In between, I guess she spoke to the big man. Parker Laing came out of the house, so he must have been in there with her when the big man left.'

'Just who is this 'big man' you're talking about? Wasn't his name mentioned?'

Bywater's smile was weary. 'We thought you might enlighten us.'

Before leaving Stone's woodshed, Sugg had taken Geary's Remington Frontier .44 to replace the six-gun he'd been forced to throw in the river. Then, realizing his .45 shells were the wrong size, he'd gone the whole hog and swapped gunbelts.

After burying Geary they had left Stone's estate, swum their horses across the North Platte, and Bywater had recovered his Colt. It had then taken them an hour to ride to Saratoga.

Tom Gaines had been dozing in his chair when their horses rattled up the street and they drew rein in front of his jail. He'd walked out to meet them, stood on the plankwalk as they swung out of the saddle and, spectacles pushed up on his forehead, told them he'd stayed late pushing a pen. They were lucky to catch him, he'd said: the jail would be manned throughout the night — either by the marshal or his deputy — if there were prisoners in the cells. Otherwise, both Saratoga's lawmen would sleep at home.

It was late. After those few words with Gaines, Bywater and Sugg had crossed the street for a cold meal in the hotel's restaurant. Fifteen minutes later they were back, this time sitting in the jail's office for a much longer talk with the marshal. They'd quickly told their story. He'd listened with a raised eyebrow, but without comment.

'Why would I know this feller's name?' Gaines asked now.

'He's an impressive figure of a man. He looks wealthy; none of us in this room could afford the clothes he's wearing. And Geary told us he headed for town once we were locked up. If he's from Saratoga, you should know him; if you were here, and he came over the bridge tonight, it's possible you saw him.'

Gaines shrugged his shoulders. 'By the description, you could be talking about Andrew Stone.'

'But he's dead, you saw his body, saw him buried?'

'No shadow of a doubt.'

'All right, and we know Hank Geary's dead, but now what about Parker Laing? He left Stone's house five minutes before we did. Allow thirty more for burying Geary, and he was maybe an hour ahead of us. Did you see him?'

'I told you, I stayed behind to catch up on paper-work. With my head bent over the desk, I wasn't doing much watching.'

Bywater sat in silence, contemplatively using a match to pick a scrap of beef from between two teeth. Clarence Sugg was smoking a cigarette; waiting, with characteristic patience, for something to happen, for someone to slip up.

There was a liquid slurping sound as Tom Gaines sipped coffee. His eyes were hooded, the lids drooping. He looked tired — but was it from overwork, Bywater wondered, or the strain of circumstances? He and the two lawyers had lied, but what was the marshal's involvement with Millard and Forrest Jackson? Had Gaines been lying to protect them, or was his own career at risk because he had committed a criminal offence — either willingly, or for cash put up by the Jacksons? What exactly were the three men hiding?

Bywater sighed, and shook his head. When he spoke, it was with lowered eyes.

'It's likely we've uncovered some dirt on Millard Jackson,' he said — then quickly glanced up. Gaines had paused, cup halfway to his lips. His tired eyes were wide open, and watching.

'Seems likely he was working for mobsters in New York some fifteen years ago, and the Pinkertons helped drive him out of town,' Bywater went on, and saw Gaines noticeably relax. 'According to Marshal Kerrigan over in Fort Steele, it was about that long ago that Mill Jackson arrived in town and hung out his shingle. But what about his brother, Forrest? How long's he been in Saratoga?'

'Almost from the outset. Moved in around '80. I'd been here a couple of years.'

'Right. So you don't know how long he's been out West?'

'No way of knowing.'

'So let's surmise. Let's say, for the sake of argument, that fifteen years ago he was in New York with his brother. I think that's reasonable. But if he was, and he got out at the same time as Millard, was it voluntary, or was he forced? Is Forrest Jackson as crooked as his brother?'

'Crooked?' Gaines repeated hollowly, looking sick.

'Oh yes. And if both of them were crooks fifteen years ago . . . '

Gaines had put down his empty cup. He was clasping it with both big-knuckled hands, staring down with a brooding look on his face.

Bywater let him stew for a moment, then changed the subject.

'You had some experience as a married man, Gaines?'

The marshal looked up, frowning, clearly wondering if this was a trick in the guise of an innocent question. Sugg, too, was looking across with interest.

'A few years. You know my wife died

giving birth to Arch,' Gaines said. 'What of it?'

'How long in Saratoga?'

'I just told you: two years longer than Forrest Jackson — '

'Forget Jackson. I've moved on. I'm talking to a man who was once married, and has been in Saratoga — a very small town — for twelve years. What I want to know is, if your wife had lived and you'd needed a birthday present, or an anniversary present, here in Saratoga — where would you have gone?'

'Mike Carey's.'

'The general store?'

'Sure. He's got a catalogue. I'd look through it, order what I wanted, after a few weeks the goods get shipped in.'

'Everybody does that?'

'That, or ride to Rawlins, or across the mountains to Laramie.'

'Yeah, well, I guess most take the easy option.' Bywater flashed a look at Sugg, and winked.

'One more question, Marshal, which sort of follows on.'

'Fire away.'

'It's after midnight. The hotel's just across the street, but our blankets are even closer, and as we've been talking of easy options . . . '

'Yeah, right,' Tom Gaines said, climbing to his feet, 'You're welcome to use two of the empty cells.' A glint of humour flared in his tired eyes. 'I'll leave the cells open. Don't forget to blow out the light.'

★ ★ ★

After the marshal had gone they made mockery of the easy option by walking their horses across the street to the livery barn and leaving them in the care of Ellery Cole. They emerged moments later, glanced up the street and saw Tom Gaines hurrying towards the saloon. Then, carrying blanket rolls, it was back to the same cells, the same open space, the same table, but instead of striped sunlight falling across its boards a smoking oil lamp cast a pool

155

of light that leaked over the table's edge but barely crawled across the floor to the two Pinkerton men.

Sugg, lying on the cornhusk mattress with his hands again clasped behind his head, said, 'What was all that about?'

'If Elizabeth Stone is Nathan Wedge's fancy woman, he'll have been giving her presents. We now know the only place he can get them in Saratoga is through Mike Carey's general store.'

'Right. But there'll be a general store in Fort Steele, maybe even a shop selling jewellery. Wedge assists in the town's bank. Why not get them on his trips there, and reduce the risk of being caught?'

'I'm banking on him going for the easy option.'

'Banking!' Sugg grinned. 'So, tomorrow morning you're going to trot across to Carey's general store, flash your badge, and demand details of all the luxury items Wedge has ordered in the past . . . what, eighteen months?'

'To be on the safe side. Then I'm

going to talk to Wedge's wife, ask her if the gold necklace was for her, if she was enchanted with the pearl ear-rings her husband bought for her — '

'If she's a loyal wife, looking at a husband heading for the US Senate — she'll lie.'

'A Pinkerton man,' Bywater said, 'cannot easily be fooled.'

14

Marshal Tom Gaines did not go straight to his bed. Instead, he strode up the street to the saloon, dragged his son Arch away from Ike Adams's bar and walked him unsteadily all the way through the town and across the bridge to the office of Forrest Jackson. As was often the case, the lawyer was burning the midnight oil. His brother, Millard, was with him.

Once inside the office, door shut, curtains closed and everyone seated, Gaines didn't beat about the bush.

'That second Pinkerton man — '

'Sugg,' Forrest said.

'Yeah, well, he's killed Hank Geary, down at the Stone place. The Pinkertons are getting too close, they already know too damn much.'

Forrest Jackson was unruffled. 'I doubt it. They cannot connect us to the dead Floyd Loomis. And nobody but the four of us in this room knows the story behind Gus Allman and that court case.'

'They can get to me and Arch through you. That must not happen.'

'What the hell have they found out that makes you think it might?'

'Something your brother could have predicted if he'd kept his goddamn wits about him: Temple Bywater knows Mill was in New York.'

'Jesus Christ,' Millard breathed. 'Are you telling me Bywater was with the Pinkertons fifteen years ago?'

'He didn't say that; it looks likely. But he does know the Pinks drove you out of town. That means they've already got enough to scupper your chances of getting that senatorship.'

'And we've lost our hired gunman,' Forrest pointed out.

Millard scowled. He walked around his brother, splashed whiskey into a glass, went and stood with his back to the curtained window.

'I'll never understand why Parker Laing finished off Loomis. If he and Geary really were working for Wedge, by killing Bywater, Loomis was saving them a job.'

'Laing's a cold-blooded killer,' Gaines said flatly. 'Loomis was already down, plugged in the shoulder by Bywater. Laing couldn't resist. We don't know the full story, and only some of the circumstances. My guess is the summer storm was the only thing that prevented Laing going on to kill Bywater.'

'There's still time,' Arch Gaines said, his speech thickened by drink. 'Geary's gone, but Laing's still hanging around.'

'Good to hear you come into the conversation, Arch,' Mill Jackson said sarcastically. 'Perhaps you can tell us how a man working for the opposition is of benefit to us.'

'Dead is dead, no matter who pulls the trigger — ' He broke off. Tom Gaines was nodding in agreement.

'Arch has got a point. More so because there's a chance Nathan Wedge will call off Laing and take himself out of the race. From what Bywater told me, he and Sugg had a brush with Bradley Wynne. If Wynne's shown his hand, Wedge may have no choice but to withdraw.'

'Well, I'm damned if that's going to happen to me,' Millard Jackson said. 'My past stays buried. Something's got to be done about Temple Bywater, and fast.'

Forrest spread his hands. 'Arch has already come up with the answer: if Wedge no longer needs Parker Laing, we use him.'

'I've got a better idea,' Millard said tightly, and he turned to glare at Arch Gaines.

Tom Gaines stood up, scowling. 'Goddamn it, Mill, Arch is a respected deputy marshal — '

'Now he is,' Millard Jackson cut in, 'but it wasn't always that way. I remember a time when your son was engaged in a much less salubrious occupation — and for what we did for

161

him, he owes us.'

'Be damned, he does! You got your settlement up front.'

'Up front, yes,' Millard said, grinning wickedly, 'but nobody said it was full and final.'

Gaines's face was pale with anger. 'Lawyers!' He almost spat the word, but Millard Jackson was unfazed.

'What d'you say, Arch?' he said. 'Finish Bywater, and permanently erase my memory of your . . . aberration?'

'What the hell's that?'

Millard chuckled. 'Doesn't matter. What is it, yes or no?'

'Tell him you'll do it,' Tom Gaines gritted. He turned and walked towards the door. 'In full and final settlement.'

'Done,' Millard Jackson said. And then, with what appeared to be sudden misgivings, he looked at Arch and said, 'You up to this? You can handle it without bungling and making matters worse than they are now?'

The deputy nodded. 'Tomorrow, first thing,' he said, and followed his father unsteadily out of the office.

'He'd better be right,' Millard Jackson said to his brother. 'I'm heading back to Fort Steele tonight. The news from Washington should be through tomorrow. I'm convinced it will be good, and when I get back here I don't want it ruined by hearing that Pinkerton man's still alive, and in Saratoga.'

15

The next morning, Bywater and Sugg waited for Marshal Gaines and his son to come clomping into the jail, smothering huge yawns, then crossed the street and ate a greasy breakfast in the café.

Sitting back over their third cup of coffee and a cigarette, Bywater surprised Sugg with an idea that had come to him during the night. Even with the oil lamp out and stars twinkling outside the high barred window, the frustrations of the investigation had been keeping sleep at bay. One overriding thought he couldn't get rid of was that something was staring him in the face, but for the life of him he couldn't see it. What was needed, he'd decided, was a fresh appraisal of the current situation by an experienced and uncluttered mind.

'Ride south,' he told Sugg. 'Talk to

Texas Jack Logan.'

'What if he's out tending traps?'

'Hunt him down. He'll thank you for it. The man's an investigator at heart. Didn't you notice the animation in his face during that talk in his cabin?'

'I saw him get fed up and walk out.'

'Just my point. We were getting nowhere, and he could see it. Now you're going to ask for his help.'

That settled it. They drained their cups, left behind the greasy smell of the café for the fresh air and bright sunlight of the street, and Bywater accompanied Sugg to Ellery Cole's to collect the lean Pinkerton man's horse.

Once mounted, Sugg waved a carefree hand, rode through the dust to join the wagons already trundling through the town, and headed down the street towards the river crossing. There he would turn towards the south, and ride the ten miles upstream to Texas Jack Logan's cabin.

Bywater stood for a moment by the pump, soaking up the early morning warmth while allowing his eyes and thoughts to wander. He had pretty well forgotten about Parker Laing since asking Tom Gaines if he'd seen the gunslinger ride back into town. Now, his wandering gaze alighted on a dark, stocky figure standing in front of the saloon and looking down the street towards Bywater.

In town but walking free, Bywater mused — and for a moment considered walking across to the jail to inform Gaines. But what was the point? If it came down to a confrontation, it was Laing's word against his. That was supposing Gaines acted on the information. Bywater was still unsure where the marshal's loyalties lay, or whether to believe even half of what he said . . .

'In a contemplative mood, Bywater?'

Forrest Jackson had approached silently, a derby hat perched on his white hair, black suit glossy in the bright sunlight and his long nose almost twitching with curiosity.

'But not getting very far.' Bywater

nodded at the lawyer's briefcase. 'And you, you're off to work?'

'Indeed. Another day at the office.'

'Righting wrongs,' Bywater said, stirring the waters with deliberate intent. Then, as a sudden thought occurred, he went further. 'I wonder if you were ever involved with the man called Floyd Loomis?'

Jackson's eyes were unreadable. 'Are you asking me if I hired that one-eyed villain to fill you full of lead?'

'Depends on how you interpret involvement,' Bywater said. He let Jackson mull on that, then said, 'Take me, for example. Fifteen years ago I was involved in a Pinkerton operation in New York City. And that raises some interesting questions. How deep was my involvement? How close did I get to some very shady characters?' He grinned. 'How much, and how many names do I remember?'

'When you've got the answers,' Forrest Jackson said, 'be sure to let me know. But don't waste too much time chasing rumour and speculation. You were brought here to investigate a murder, not blacken the names of prominent citizens.'

Feeling smug, Bywater watched the little man stalk off on his way to the river crossing and his office, then walked the few yards down the street to Michael Carey's general store.

★ ★ ★

The cool, shadowy store smelled strongly of kerosene and lye soap, the drier odour of grain and potatoes in hemp sacks, the subtler scents of the delicate soaps and bottled perfumes Carey kept in stock for the ladies of Saratoga.

A petite, middle-aged woman wearing a long skirt, white shirt with puffed sleeves and a scarf to protect her head from the sun, was turning away from the counter with her purchases when Bywater walked in. She looked at him with unusual interest — his presence and reason for being in town had not gone unnoticed, he thought wryly — then walked past him without haste and left the store.

Carey was stout enough to expand to bursting point his faded bib-and-brace overalls. His face was red. Perspiration beaded his brow.

'Too damn hot, too damn early,' he complained to Bywater, as he went behind the counter and perched himself on a stool. 'Teamster rolls up with his wagon before I'm fully awake, I've helped unload a ton of goods before the first customer walks in.'

'Take a breather. I've come to talk, not buy.'

'Thought as much. You're that Pinkerton man. The one who shot Gus Allman.'

'Think of me instead as the man looking into Andrew Stone's murder, and possible corruption linked to the re-election.'

'How's that again?'

'Candidates may not be as clean as

they look. That's where you come in.'

'Hah! I mind my own business. Serving everything from soap to shotgun cartridges doesn't leave much time for spying on crooked politicians.'

'But you do keep records? I'm interested in catalogue sales. Do you keep a record of what people order, and the dates ordered?'

'Sure. But those records are confidential . . . '

He trailed off as Bywater reached into his vest pocket and placed his Pinkerton badge face up on the counter.

'That badge gives me the right to look.'

There was a heavy silence. A wagon trundled by, mules snorting. A whip cracked. Dust drifted in through the open doorway. Someone laughed shrilly. Carey lifted his head as footsteps thumped on the boards. He looked beyond Bywater and said, 'Later, Mrs Crane, I'm tied up for a few minutes,' then returned his gaze to Bywater and met the Pinkerton man's patient, penetrating stare.

He sighed extravagantly, shook his head with obvious displeasure, then reached under the counter and came up with a heavy book.

'What do you want to know?'

'What luxury items has Nathan Wedge ordered in the past eighteen months?'

Carey rolled his eyes. 'Be more precise.'

'Jewellery. Necklaces, lockets, bracelets. Or it could be a lady's purse, fancy shoes . . . '

As Bywater spoke, the storekeeper was thumbing through the pages. He frowned, dug into his bib pocket and perched a pair of spectacles on his nose. He leaned closer to the book.

'Too early,' he grunted. 'Nothing eighteen months back. Nothing fourteen' — he flicked the pages — 'thirteen . . . Then twelve months ago he began ordering on a regular basis. Luxury items.' He looked up defiantly. 'For Mrs Wedge.'

'Once a month?'

Carey grunted. 'Just about. And that last was a good guess of yours. The latest was a pair of fancy patent leather shoes, ordered last month.'

'Arrived?'

'Yesterday.'

'I'll take them.'

'No. There's a limit: that I *can't* allow.'

'When I leave here, I'm going to the bank. I'll give them to Wedge.' Bywater smiled, hoping to inspire confidence. 'After that I'm going to see his wife. He and I are on friendly terms. He might ask me to take them to her.'

Another extravagant sigh. A quick look across towards the door, and the realization that the impatient Mrs Crane had been joined by other impatient customers. With a shake of the head, Carey weaved his way through crates and sacks and stacks of cans to the back of the store, and returned carrying a rectangular parcel which he handed to Bywater.

172

'If you'd spoken up earlier,' he said grumpily, 'you could've saved yourself a journey, spoken to her *and* given her these without leaving the store.' He caught Bywater's puzzled look and said, 'That was Diane Wedge who walked past you as you came in. It was her buckboard you heard rattling off up the street.'

16

Bywater had not heard the buckboard, and he had no intention of talking to Wedge. At least, not yet. Instead, he walked out of the store with his parcel and crossed the street to the jail. There he learned the location of the banker's house, thanked Gaines for the information and went back across the street to Cole's livery barn to pick up Doone.

He kept his eyes skinned, looking in all directions through eye-watering clouds of dust as he threaded his way between lumbering wagons and ranch hands mounted on frisky horses moving swiftly up and down the street. His apparent fear of getting knocked down and trampled was hiding the real purpose of his scrutiny, which was to determine the whereabouts of Parker Laing.

When he reached the opposite plank-walk without locating the dangerous gunman, he experienced the first twinge of regret for sending Clarence Sugg south to Texas Jack Logan's cabin. He was about to swap the comparative safety of Saratoga for the exposure of the open country, and he could have done with the tall Pinkerton man's experienced backup.

No matter. What's done was done. He walked quickly down the livery barn's runway, and five minutes later the parcel was safe in his saddle-bag and he was riding out of town in the general direction of Medicine Bow Peak.

It took him thirty minutes to reach the neat cabin owned by Nathan Wedge. The banker's home was on high ground from where the outskirts of Saratoga could be seen through the heat-haze, half hidden by a grove of aspen, a white picket fence enclosing a neat front garden.

Bywater approached it at a trot, musing at the way a spell of uninterrupted thought during the short ride had seen his plans change. He had set out with the intention of confronting Diane Wedge with a barrage of questions designed to leave her flustered and, in the confusion, letting slip secrets that might incriminate her husband. Instead, he knew that if he played his cards right there would be no need for the direct approach. What he carried in his saddle would be enough to cause the banker's wife — without prompting, without any idea of Bywater's true intentions — to hammer the final nail in the coffin containing her husband's political ambitions.

The buckboard Carey had mentioned was at the side of the cabin. The horse had been taken out of harness and could be seen trotting across the small corral behind the house. Bywater rode up to the picket fence, swung down and ground-hitched Doone. Then, carrying the parcel, he made his way through the gate and knocked on the front door.

Diane Wedge's eyebrows rose when she saw who had come calling.

'Mr Bywater?'

'Twice in less than an hour,' Bywater said, straight-faced. 'I wonder which one of us should feel honoured?'

That brought a bright, cautious smile. 'That would be me, of course,' she said. 'After all, you're a famous Pinkerton operative. But then I have to ask you why you're here, and at once I start feeling flustered for no apparent reason and — '

'May I come in?'

'Is it necessary?'

'Well, it's quite possible your husband is heading for the US Senate, and I'd be honoured to get to know his charming wife. But that's not the real reason I'm here.' He held up the parcel. 'I'm delivering a present.'

'What . . . for me?'

He nodded.

'And you're not going to ask questions about Andrew Stone's murder?'

'I hadn't planned to,' Bywater said, mentally crossing his fingers.

Again the brilliant smile, now much

less hesitant. 'Do come on in.'

He followed her into a bright living room, confirming as he did so the impression he had got in Carey's store: Diane Wedge was much smaller and daintier than Elizabeth Stone. And that, Bywater thought, was why questions were unnecessary, and why Nathan Wedge's guilt would be established by one inevitable response he was sure to get from Mrs Wedge.

She sat him down on a chair, and brought him a cold lemon drink from the kitchen. Then she perched opposite him.

Bywater had placed the parcel on the floor. Her glance flicked towards it, then back to Bywater.

'You recall seeing me in the general store?' She nodded. 'While I was there, I picked up that parcel from Mike Carey. It's a present for you. From Nathan.'

'But there's no name on it; no writing at all.'

'Nevertheless . . . '

She was biting her lip. Her cheeks were pink, her eyes sparkling.

'Goodness,' she said. 'Nathan is a fine man, a wonderful husband — but he never, ever walks in with a surprise present.'

'Doesn't he?' Bywater said innocently, remembering Mike Carey with glasses perched on his nose as he listed Wedge's orders and realizing that with her last words this woman had already given him everything he needed. All except the proof . . .

'Do you know what it is?' she said.

'Open it and see.'

He passed her the parcel. She held it for a moment, her eyes dancing. Then she ripped off the brown paper. The shoe box was revealed. She lifted the lid, carefully took out one of the black shoes and turned it so that brilliant spots of sunlight reflected by the shiny patent leather danced across walls and ceiling.

'But these are very large,' she said, frowning. 'Much too big for me.

Nathan knows my size. If he really has bought me a pair of shoes, these are not they.' She smiled apologetically. 'I'm sorry, Mr Bywater, but I'm afraid Mike Carey's given you the wrong parcel.'

★   ★   ★

The skies had clouded over when Bywater approached Saratoga, and a fine drizzle was falling. He rode past an unkempt area of wasteland where the detritus of the town had been dumped to rot, and was pushing up the gentle slope to where the road crested a hump and dipped into the town proper when he saw the Indian-dark figure of Arch Gaines knee his rangy buckskin out of an alley and sit waiting. A deputy's badge glittered on his vest. As Bywater drew closer he saw that the young man's countenance was bleak, his black eyes darting nervously in all directions.

Bywater drew alongside the deputy and nodded a greeting. He was about to ride on by when, without warning,

Gaines dipped a hand to his holster and drew his six-gun. He cocked the hammer, and pointed the weapon at Bywater.

'Hold it there. Orders from my pa. You're to come with me.'

Bywater turned Doone on a dime, looked at the levelled six-gun.

'You're shaking, partner.'

Something like panic flared in the dark eyes. The six-gun jerked, indicating the alley behind the deputy.

'Down there. You lead, I'll follow.'

'How can I lead,' Bywater said, 'when I don't know where I'm going?'

'I want you in front of me, so there's no funny business.'

'Or is it,' Bywater said, 'so you can shoot me in the back?'

A nervous smile twitched. The young Gaines bit his lower lip, and Bywater's skin prickled. *Christ! Had he hit on the truth?*

'Move,' Gaines said.

'Why you? I was expecting Parker Laing.'

'Forget Laing, he's left town.'

For a moment, Bywater hesitated. There was nobody about. The hump in the road and beyond it the slope into town ensured that nothing could be seen but the tops of rickety false fronts pointing to the leaden skies. It was a slack time. If any goods wagons were due, they had arrived early. They would be unloading, and would leave in the afternoon.

Bywater was on his own, held at gunpoint, and with no help in sight.

Clenching his teeth, he touched Doone with his heels and brushed past Gaines close enough to rattle stirrups. The fleeting thought that hit him hard as he rode by was that this could be his last chance: a fast sweeping blow with one hand would knock the pistol out of the deputy's hand; once past and in front of the lawman, he was finished.

Then the slim chance had slipped away, and it was too late.

The alley ran straight ahead for thirty yards, then turned left. Bywater guessed it was now running parallel to the main street, and that was confirmed almost at once when he glanced up another intersecting alley and found himself looking straight through the open door of Ike Adams's saloon — across the main street, a ridiculously short forty yards away that might as well have been forty miles.

The horses' hoofs were beginning to slip on thin surface mud as the drizzle took effect. The breeze had picked up. There was a chill to the rain. Bywater lifted a hand to turn up his collar, and drew a sharp warning from Gaines. Ignoring him, he tugged his hat down, and pushed on.

Then the rough timber buildings on the right of the alley petered out to give way to the same open area of scrub across which the rain was drifting like thin mist. At the same time Bywater became aware of the musical ring of a blacksmith's hammer. Ahead of him, blue smoke issued from an open fronted shed to mingle with the rain. As

Bywater drew level and the tang of smoke and hot metal bit into his nostrils, he saw the white-hot glow of a furnace, the showers of sparks as the big hammer rose and fell to shape the glowing strip of iron the blacksmith was holding on the anvil with the aid of huge pincers.

A big man, Bywater noticed — but aren't blacksmiths always big? He saw the movement of the man's head, attracted by the sound of their passing, the glint of eyes glowing a devilish red in the furnaces reflected light. He thought of yelling to the man, wondered for an instant at the reaction that might draw from Gaines, whether he would die with the words still spilling from his lips — and then, once again, the moment had passed.

Suddenly, ten yards on, Gaines was crowding him, urging his horse hard against Doone, pushing from behind.

'Move,' he said, his voice tight, 'Move, move — '

'Arch, what the hell's going on?'

Bywater looked up to the grey sky, uttered a silent prayer — and drew the big black mare to a halt.

Another moment lost, another chance gone, he thought. But this time it's Gaines who's in trouble. He's left it too late. He can't shoot now, not with the big man watching. And, by God, I'll make damn sure there's no second chance.

'Arch?'

'Back off, Ty. I'm taking this feller in.'

'What the hell d'you mean, taking him in?'

The blacksmith had left his shop, but not the pincers or the glowing strip of metal. It was hissing in the rain. Puffs of steam were gusting back into his bearded face.

'He's the man who shot Gus Allman.'

'I know that. I also know he works for the Pinkertons — and if you're taking him in for some damn reason, then you've lost your sense of direction. Only place this'll take you is the river, and you know it.'

'Yeah, well . . . '

'I thought you'd finished with this craziness five years ago?'

'Goddammit to hell!'

With a sudden flurry of movement the deputy spun his horse, lashed it with the loose end of the reins and urged it past the blacksmith's bulk. He rode so close the hot metal hissed along the horse's flank, and there was a sudden stink of burning hair. Then he was gone, pounding back up the alley with the six-gun still glittering in his fist, mud spraying from beneath his mount's flying hoofs.

'My turn to ask the questions,' Bywater said as silence settled. 'What the hell was all that about?'

The big man grinned, showing teeth like gleaming alabaster tombstones.

'Saw you go past, saw the six-gun in his fist — and what I told him was right: this alley goes straight down to the North Platte, with no cut offs.'

'At the outset, he told me he was acting on his pa's orders.'

'If he was, there's something mighty

funny going on.'

He turned to walk back to his workshop. Bywater walked Doone alongside him.

'What happened five years ago?'

Massive shoulders shrugged. 'There was an armed robbery out near Laramie, talk of young Arch in deep. He must have been what, sixteen, seventeen? Thereabouts. Anyway, he looked certain to take a fall. Then, overnight, everything changed. Another man was charged, and convicted.'

'Don't tell me,' Bywater said. 'The trial was in Fort Steele, Mill Jackson the defence lawyer.'

The blacksmith nodded.

'And since then Arch Gaines has been clean?'

'Sure. His pa took him on as deputy — probably so's he could keep an eye on him, dawn to dusk. Seems it worked, too.'

He ducked in out of the rain, clanged the iron back on the anvil and turned to squint back at Bywater.

'If you ask me,' he said, 'you were looking at an early grave somewhere out in that wet scrub. Arch Gaines was about to commit murder. There must be a hell of a lot at stake.'

'Oh, there is,' Bywater said. 'But thanks to you, I'm now a lot closer to clearing up this whole mess.'

17

One of the questions Temple Bywater had been unable to answer was why Gus Allman had been paying Forrest Jackson regular visits. But his talk with the blacksmith had changed all that.

If Forrest and his brother Mill had conspired to make sure another man was convicted of Arch Gaines's crime, then that man — surely Gus Allman? — would not only be seeking revenge when he walked out of jail, he would be carrying with him a deadly weapon. That weapon was the knowledge of malpractice, and the threat of exposure. It was a short jump from there to the obvious conclusion that Gus Allman had been blackmailing Forrest Jackson. He had been calling at the lawyer's office to collect his money.

Obvious, yes — but the answer led to another question: why had the Jackson brothers, both respectable lawyers, protected Arch Gaines? Why had Mill Jackson allowed Gus Allman to be sent to prison for a crime he did not commit?'

Again, the answer was obvious: Marshal Tom Gaines had arrested Gus Allman for a crime his son committed, ensured Mill Jackson was taken on as Allman's lawyer, then paid him to make a hash of the defence; a respectable lawyer had accepted a bribe.

The blackmail was easily proved by a close examination of Forrest Jackson's bank account. And all that was required was a heart-to-heart talk with an indiscreet banker who was in no position to take the moral high ground.

Damp but exhilarated, Bywater took the narrow intersecting alley, crossed the street and hitched Doone outside the saloon. Before going in, he paused for a moment to glance down the street. He was hoping to see Clarence Sugg's horse hitched somewhere — outside the jail, or the café — but it was nowhere to be seen. Disappointed, he slapped rain-water off his hat, walked up to the bar and ordered a drink.

Ike Adams was watching him with a perceptive eye.

'Looks like the cat got the cream.'

'He can smell it,' Bywater said.

'You saying you know who killed Stone?'

'Not that, no. But I think I know why Gus Allman was visiting Forrest Jackson from the time he got out of the pen.'

'For certain? With proof?'

Bywater grinned. 'You should be a Pinkerton op,' he said, then turned serious and pursed his lips. 'If I'm right, I'll have that proof in half-an-hour.'

'And where will that lead you?'

'To a serious pow-wow with Forrest Jackson and Tom Gaines.'

'*Gaines?*' Adams said, eyebrows raised in surprise.

He opened his mouth to ask what Bywater knew would be the first of many more questions. Quickly, Bywater drained his glass and turned to leave.

On his way out, another thought struck him. He stopped and looked back.

'The name of the man replacing Andrew Stone will be announced very soon. How will it reach here?'

Adams looked uncertain. 'You're talking to the man running the saloon, not someone in high office. My guess would be a wire from Washington to Rawlins, one for each candidate. When that happens, it's likely we'll see Mill Jackson riding in to deliver the news that he's off to the senate.'

'You could be right,' Bywater said, 'but if the talk with his brother goes the way I think it will, poetic justice will quickly wipe the smile off his face.'

And, leaving the saloonist frowning, he pushed through the doors and walked out into the grey, wet street.

* * *

When Temple Bywater walked into the Saratoga bank, it was empty of customers. Behind the counter an elderly teller with thinning grey hair was working on his own, bent over as he skilfully counted a wad of banknotes. He looked up as Bywater came in, waited expectantly with one hand holding the notes down, the other ready to resume counting.

'Wedge in?'

'He's in his office. Whom should I say is calling?'

'Would you tell him Temple Bywater would like to talk to him — in private.'

The teller looked about him, and seemed surprised to see that there was nobody there to help him. With a quick glance at Bywater he stowed the wad of notes in a drawer, trotted away to knock on a door at the back of the room, opened it and poked his head around. He listened for a moment, then withdrew, carefully left the door ajar and returned to the counter.

'Go through, Mr Bywater. Mr Wedge will see you now.'

Wedge's office was small and dim.

He remained seated behind his desk as Bywater walked in. Indicating a chair, he waited until Bywater was seated. Then he sprang to the attack.

'Have you established who murdered Andrew Stone?'

'Not yet.'

'Why not? Do you realize every day that goes by without an arrest means one more day during which people look on me with suspicion?'

'You, and Millard Jackson.'

'Indeed.' Wedge was almost sneering. 'But Jackson's always been a crook, and could well be guilty.'

'You're all guilty in one way or another — and guilty men don't get elected to the senate.'

Wedge sat back. He was frowning, his fingers drumming on the desk; the veneer of steel Bywater had noticed in Texas Jack's cabin seemed to have developed cracks.

'I told you: I did not murder Andrew Stone, nor did I arrange his murder.'

'That remains to be seen. But you

certainly sent a gunman after me.'

'You cannot prove that.'

'Why? Because Loomis is dead?' Bywater smiled. 'Doesn't matter. I don't need that proof, because you'd slipped up long before you hired a killer. You've been transgressing, Wedge, breaking strict moral codes and not even bothering to hide your tracks.'

'What the hell does that mean?'

'It means I know about your philandering.'

The fingers stopped their insistent drumming. Wedge's mouth had fallen open. He licked his lips. The veneer of steel had split wide open.

'I don't know what you mean — '

'Elizabeth Stone. Name ring a bell?'

'Andrew Stone's widow? Of course I know the name.'

'Oh, you know much more than that. I'd say you've been very familiar with her.'

'Nonsense. You're making more wild accusations, again without a shred of proof — '

'Really? Earlier today, I was talking to Mike Carey, over at the store. We looked through his order books. It was very enlightening. I was impressed. So impressed I thought it might be reasonable to ask your wife if she'd appreciated all those expensive presents.'

'You did that!' Suddenly Wedge's voice was hoarse.

'No, I did *better* than that. Your latest present of a pair of shoes had arrived, as perhaps you know. So I delivered it to her.'

Wedge groaned. He leaned forward, dropped his head into his hands. He remained that way for several long seconds. When he finally looked up, his face was grey.

'What do you want?'

'Andrew Stone, an elected senator, was murdered. Odds are the killing was arranged by you or Millard Jackson — '

'I *told* you — '

'Yes, all right. But since arriving in Saratoga, there have been attempts on my life. I blame you, and I blame Mill Jackson. But what were your motives? At first I thought it was to stop me finding out who murdered Stone, but with both of you trying to kill me, that didn't make sense. So I decided two candidates for the senatorship were trying to hide some pretty nasty skeletons lurking in dark cupboards — skeletons that would ruin your chances of making it to the senate. In your case I've been proved right, haven't I? Now it's Mill Jackson's turn.'

Bywater paused.

'You asked me what I want. Well, I believe the news from Washington will come by wire to Rawlins — is that right?' Wedge nodded. 'Have you got a man in Rawlins?'

'Yes. That's why Percy's on his own out there. A young cashier's been hanging around the Rawlins telegraph office for the past two days.'

'Then I must have seen him.' Bywater shrugged. 'Never mind. When he brings that wire here, and if it's your ticket to the senate, I expect you to send him straight back to Rawlins or Fort Steele carrying a wire, from you, regretfully refusing the senatorship — '

Bywater held up a hand as a distraught Wedge half rose from his chair.

'You'll do it. The alternatives, both here for a respected bank manager, and elsewhere for a man newly elected to the senate, must be too dreadful to contemplate.' Bywater let that sink in, then said, 'But that could be some hours away. Right now I want your help.'

'And why should I give it?'

'Because if your chance of a seat on the senate is dead and buried, I'm quite sure you would like to see Mill Jackson stopped. A quick look through his bank accounts for the last six months will give me the ammunition to do that.'

There was a thin film of perspiration on the banker's pale brow. The fingers that had been tapping were now trembling. He suddenly became aware of the shaking, and clasped his hands. He shook his head despairingly.

'There's no need to look at them,' he said. 'I'm well aware that Jackson has been drawing out a small cash sum on the first of every month. Those withdrawals began shortly after Gus Allman got out of jail and returned to Saratoga.' He smiled bitterly at Bywater. 'Yes, I know what's been going on. And I'm quite sure that if I'd made the knowledge public, everybody — especially his father, the town mayor — would have understood why Jackson was paying money to an ex-con. But I couldn't do that, could I? When a man's got a dark secret, he doesn't dash around town pointing an accusing finger.'

He paused, his eyes suddenly haunted. They were the eyes of a man who has held a dream cupped like a sparrow in the palms of his hands, and watched it flutter away.

'When you . . . take this to the

Jackson . . . keep my name out of it
— if you can.'

Bywater nodded. 'I owe you that much.'

'When will you confront them?'

'I'm on my way.'

18

As Bywater urged Doone down the street towards the bridge over the North Platte, a young rider on a mud-spattered pony galloped towards him and swept on by. He was followed by a buckboard that came bouncing and rattling up the gentle slope. A big, bearded man was in the seat, straw hair blowing in the wet breeze. He saw Bywater, lifted a hand and roared a greeting. Then he too was gone, leaving a shower of mud in his wake.

A hundred yards further on, a paint pony came splashing towards him through the mud. It was Clarence Sugg. The Pinkerton man saw Bywater and swung the pony across the street.

'Millard Jackson's in town,' he said as the two horses came together, steaming in the cool, damp air. 'I was nearing the bridge, following Texas Jack downriver, when I saw him on the opposite bank. He was heading this way at a hell of a lick. Looked like he was coming from Fort Steele. He rode into the town, then turned away from the bridge and hammered down the street towards his brother's office.'

'I'd say the wire he was waiting for arrived in Forte Steele.'

'There were two riders,' Sugg said, 'the second one close behind Jackson.'

'That would be the young feller who passed me, heading up towards the bank. Wedge had a cashier waiting in Rawlins. That would be him. So we can safely say each man now knows if he's won, or lost.'

'But the way these contests are run, the successful candidate will be announced separately. The one who's lost won't know who beat him.'

'With just the two candidates, it won't be difficult to work out.' Bywater shrugged. 'They were finished anyway. Everything's fallen into place. We've got enough to guarantee that, no matter what those wires say, their political ambitions are on the scrap heap.'

But Sugg's mind was elsewhere.

'Did you see Texas Jack?'

'He passed me, gave me a yell on his way up town. Does that mean he's helped the investigation along?'

'That's what I went for, but I didn't get around to asking him.' Sugg pulled a face. 'I spent some time alone in Jack's cabin, when he was out tending his traps. I spotted something, and when I took a closer look I knew there was a big problem.'

Bywater frowned. 'In what way?'

'Well, it could be something, or nothing — '

'Then it can wait.'

Anxious to get after the Jacksons — especially now he knew Millard was in town — Bywater made his statement flat, and final. Sugg slid a gloved hand across the wet saddle horn, rubbed absently with his finger, thought for a moment.

'Sure,' he said. 'I don't think Texas

Jack's going anywhere.'

'Then turn your horse around. We're going to see Forrest Jackson. If Mill came bearing good news, we're about to ruin the party.'

They clattered west over the bridge. As they rode the few hundred yards across open space to the wide street where the lawyer's office was situated, Bywater hurriedly brought Sugg up to date. He began with his visit to the general store, went on to his visit to Diane Wedge, the brush with Arch Gaines and his confrontation with Nathan Wedge in the Saratoga bank.

The lanky Pinkerton man nodded his approval, but immediately spotted the danger.

'Arch Gaines left you in a panic, after showing his hand. He would have gone straight to his pa. You're not only about to ruin the Jacksons, you're going to do the same to Tom and Arch Gaines. You think two crooked lawmen will stand for that?'

'Damn. I passed the jail, didn't see

them there, should've checked.'

'Tom Gaines is smart. He bribed a lawyer, but he'll know he's safe if he can eliminate any proof he was involved in wrongdoing. And he'll do that by going to the men he bribed, and making sure they keep their mouths shut.'

'I can see that — and there's only one sure way of doing it.' Bywater said grimly.

'Yes, and it's easy for a town marshal to concoct a plausible story,' Sugg said. 'He found out Gus Allman's conviction was a miscarriage of justice. He went with Arch to arrest the lawyers involved. They resisted. In the ensuing gun battle, both men died. Done that way, they'd be in the clear.'

'Not quite,' Bywater said grimly. 'They'd still have us to contend with.'

'We'd struggle proving anything, with Gus Allman and the two lawyers dead.' He looked sideways at Bywater. 'Besides,' he said, 'aren't we losing sight of the fact that we came here to unmask Andrew Stone's killer?'

'No, we're not,' Bywater said. 'Because there's a good chance that killer is a lawyer, or a lawman.'

He missed Sugg's sceptical glance, because they were rapidly approaching Forrest Jackson's office. They had reached the side alley down which Gaines had led Bywater on his first visit. Bywater drew rein there and sat for a moment, enduring the cold drizzle as he tried to out-think the two lawmen.

There were several people about: a man and a woman leaving Joe Ringling's yard and climbing into a buggy, a horseman with the rough attire and leisurely demeanour of a drifter, another man sweeping up outside what looked like a gunsmith's shop.

Bywater could see four horses tied at the hitch rail in front of Forrest Jackson's office. He recognized Arch Gaines's rangy buckskin from their earlier encounter, and remembered seeing the other horse, a palomino, tied up outside the jail when he rode into Saratoga with Gus Allman's body. It was almost certainly Tom Gaines's horse, which meant the marshal and his deputy were inside Jackson's office. But having established that they were there, as Bywater had been half expecting — what did they intend to do?

'How will Gaines and his boy work it, Bony?'

'Plugging the lawyers inside their office would do the job — and disposing of the bodies is easy, because the undertaker's just across the street.' Sugg frowned, then shook his head.

'So what don't you like?'

'I think they'd prefer to have one or two reliable witnesses prepared to state that it was a clean, legal killing.'

'So they get the Jacksons out in the open — '

'And move them towards town.'

'Yeah.' Bywater nodded. 'Two lawmen, two prisoners.'

'Setting out for the jail,' Sugg said, his eyes cold, 'but with never a hope in hell of making it that far.'

And then, as if the musing of the two

Pinkerton men had been heard and taken as a signal, Forrest Jackson's door crashed open and the little lawyer stumbled out into the street. The damp wind caught his white hair. He twisted, looked back, one hand raised as if warding off evil spirits. Then an unseen pistol cracked, and mud spurted, spattering the frightened lawyer's shiny boots.

★   ★   ★

'Pull back into the alley.'

Bywater snapped the words, then followed his own advice and backed Doone into the narrow passage between the business premises. Sugg joined him, the frisky paint tossing its head and snorting uneasily. Sugg leaned forward, cupped a hand over the paint's muzzle, at the same time reaching back to ease his six-gun in its holster.

'That shot was designed to cow the Jacksons, and attract attention,' he said. 'Folks will see the lawyers led out at gunpoint. They'll put two and two together, figure they're under arrest, wonder why. When the party moves off, they'll *know* the lawyers are being taken to the jail — and those with enough morbid curiosity will follow.'

Bywater was nodding to let Sugg know he agreed, but also listening intently for sounds that would alert him to what was happening outside the alley. They came quickly. Voices, some raised, no words distinguishable. Then a horse's shrill whinny. A curse. The jingle of harness and the wet splat of hoofs in mud.

'They're coming this way now,' he warned, looking up the alley towards the street. 'The Jacksons will be in front, the two lawmen following — guns drawn. We'll let them go, then fall in behind. When they decide the time and the place is right, Tom Gaines will shout a warning — especially for the benefit of witnesses — and when we hear that . . .'

He stopped talking. With a quick glance to make sure Sugg had filled in

209

the missing words and understood what they must do, he watched Forrest Jackson ride by, then Millard Jackson, then Tom Gaines and his son. They were there, then gone, four men riding with grim intent into a situation, soon to be arranged by the two crooked lawmen, from which only two of the four would emerge with their lives.

Bywater looked at Sugg, nodded, then touched Doone with his heels and led the way out of the alley.

As they turned into the street and fell in some thirty yards behind the four riders, the rain stopped and the hot sun of early afternoon began to break up the clouds. Almost at once the heat got to work on the damp streets. Vapour began drifting about the legs of the walking horses like the tattered shreds of gun smoke. The sun glinted on the lawmen's drawn six-guns.

Ahead of the riders, the timber bridge over the North Platte river was a narrow bottleneck. Some fifty yards before the bridge the street widened and the buildings petered out, creating the wide, open space which Bywater and Sugg had crossed.

The four riders ahead of Bywater and Sugg had reached the end of the buildings. As the expanse of shiny mud beckoned, now drenched in hot sunlight, the horses caught the scent of the river and increased their pace.

At once, a powerful voice rang out.

'Deputy, they're making a run for it!'

A shot rang out. Millard Jackson's hat flew into the air. A second shot cracked, then a third, and the lawyers' horses panicked. They bolted, ears flattened. As they ran they drew rapidly apart, racing towards the far corners of the open space, the lawyers' coat tails flying as they hung on.

For a moment, Tom and Arch Gaines were nonplussed. Then the marshal roared his disbelief and chagrin and let loose a hail of bullets.

Temple Bywater flashed a tense look at Sugg, and spurred Doone forward.

'Hold your fire, Gaines,' he yelled,

bearing down on the lawman.

Gaines spun his horse, his mouth gaping in surprise. Arch Gaines had been urging his horse after Millard Jackson, who was clinging on to a careering horse threatening to carry him north along the bank of the North Platte. Now the young deputy heard Bywater's voice. He drew rein, turned, and was caught in a no man's land of indecision.

Tom Gaines recovered first. He was a lawman of vast experience. In the blink of an eye he correctly assessed the situation. His mouth set in a thin grim line, he turned his six-gun on the two Pinkerton men.

His first shot knocked Clarence Sugg out of the saddle. His second clipped Doone's cheek strap and the big black mare reared in fright. Hanging on, Bywater snapped a shot under the horse's neck. Gaines jerked backwards in the saddle, grabbed his shoulder as bright blood began to stain his shirt.

He cast a wild glance behind him,

looking for his son.

'Arch?'

But Arch Gaines had seen Sugg go down, Temple Bywater open fire and his father take a slug in the shoulder. White-faced, the young deputy tore the badge from his shirt and flung it into the drying mud, then turned his horse and spurred it across the bridge.

'So now it's just you and me,' Bywater said. He'd glanced across and seen Clarence Sugg, shaken, but on his feet and poking his foot into a stirrup. Now he moved Doone close to the marshal, his six-gun levelled at the wounded man.

'I should've known,' Gaines said through his teeth as blood trickled between his fingers. 'As soon as you arrived in town — I should have known.'

'It should have been clear long before that,' Bywater said. 'You must have realized it was over for you as soon as you paid a bribe — '

'No. None of this would have come out, *none* of it,' Gaines said, 'if Wedge and Millard Jackson hadn't got ambitious — '

'And let that ambition lead them to murder,' Bywater said. 'Which one was it, Gaines? Who was it arranged the murder of Andrew Stone?'

'Not them. Not the Jacksons, not Wedge, not me nor my boy. Stone's death gave them the opening. But they didn't kill him to create it.'

'Someone did.'

Bywater reached down, took hold of Gaines's trailing reins. Sugg had moved close, and was waiting, face pale but eyes bright. With the cessation of gunfire, the two lawyers had gained control of their horses. They'd ridden back cautiously across the open ground, and were now drawing near.

'Bony, are you strong enough to take Gaines up and lock him in his own jail?'

'Leave it to me.'

'I'll ride back with these two bright sparks,' Bywater said, raising his voice, 'see what they've got to say for themselves.'

Forrest Jackson caught his words, nodded, and rode on by with his brother. Sugg took the marshal's reins from Bywater, and set off towards the bridge. Bywater followed the lawyers.

Some of it's over, he thought, as he swung out of the saddle outside Forrest's office, *yet I'm no closer to finding the killer. And I've got a horrible feeling that, when I do, it's going to give me very little satisfaction.*

19

'As lawyers, they're finished, and they know it,' Bywater told Sugg. 'Whether they face criminal charges is up to Charlie Eames up in Denver. My guess is he'll leave them alone. It all happened five years ago, a hell of a long time in the West. We uncovered their wrongdoing as part of a different investigation. The man they allowed to be wrongly convicted is dead, and the man we believe committed the crime has left town for Christ knows where.'

The two Pinkerton men were sitting in Tom Gaines's office. The marshal was in the cell twice occupied by Clarence Sugg. Sugg was nursing a bruised shoulder: Gaines's bullet had whistled past his ear, and his instinctive sideways jerk had carried him out of the saddle to fall heavily on the packed earth.

'What about Stone's killer?'

'You heard Gaines. He told us none of them had anything to do with that. I put it to the Jacksons. They agree they seized the opportunity when Stone's death left an opening, but swear they did not create that opening.'

'And what about Nathan Wedge? He had two good reasons for wanting Stone out of the way: a chance at the senatorship, and Stone's pretty wife. Three, if you count Elizabeth as separate from the money Wedge will inherit if he marries her.'

Bywater was watching Sugg closely, and now he shook his head.

'Sure, he had all those reasons. But despite those, you don't really believe he did it — do you?'

Sugg shook his head. He was intent on rolling a cigarette. When he looked up, his face was gloomy.

'I *know* he didn't do it.'

'How? Is this what you wanted to talk about? This 'something' you spotted in Texas Jack's cabin?'

'That's right. And you'll kick yourself when I tell you, because I know you saw it. Remember the commemorative plaque he's got hanging over his bed?'

'Sure. A stone-chipping hammer. Something miners use. What about it?'

'It's not his.'

'Did he tell you, or did you read the inscription?'

'I told you. I spent time alone. He doesn't know I've looked at it.'

Bywater took a deep breath. Clarence Sugg was right. Not only was he kicking himself for not reading the inscription on the metal plate attached to the mounting board, his mind was making the extraordinary leap from a simple riverside cabin to the big white house between Saratoga and Fort Steele and coming to a terrible conclusion.

'I'm pleased about that,' Bywater said, 'because when I tackle him I'll have the advantage of surprise. I think I'll need that. Texas Jack's a tough customer.'

'If you're preparing to confront him,

you don't need me to tell you who the plaque belonged to.'

'No. I'm pretty sure it used to hang on the wall in Andrew Stone's house,' Bywater said, misery in his voice. 'Elizabeth Stone saw me looking at the blank space. She told me what hung there had been treasured by her husband. She said the man who killed her husband broke in and stole it. After all that, identifying the killer isn't too difficult. I remember Tom Gaines saying that Texas Jack was a veteran of the Pike's Peak gold-rush, but he didn't think the old-timer had ever met Andrew Stone.'

'He was wrong,' Clarence Sugg said. 'Years ago, when he was working with us, Texas Jack used to moan about the money he had, and lost. We used to believe it was strong drink doing the talking. I guess he was telling the truth — and we now know where that money went.'

'Andrew Stone stole it. And Texas Jack's waited all this time to get even. If you can call it that. Me, I wouldn't say a miserable plaque was suitable recompense for what Jack had taken from him.'

They sat in silence for a few moments. Sugg was quietly smoking. Bywater was lost in thought, from time to time looking absently out of the window.

After a while, Sugg said, 'Two members of the town council called in. As Mayor Allman's still back East with his wife, they're arranging for someone to take over as temporary town marshal. I told them I'd stay put here until the new man arrives.'

Bywater grunted.

'Millard Jackson didn't get elected,' he said. He looked across at his friend. 'I guess that means Nathan Wedge did. I'd better call in at the bank on my way to the saloon, make sure he's going to keep his word about refusing the nomination.'

'And you're going to the saloon because . . . ?'

'Texas Jack's in town,' Bywater said, climbing to his feet and hitching up his gunbelt, 'so he's going to be picking up supplies, or standing with his boots in sawdust, his elbows on a bar and a glass of whiskey in his big fist. I've been watching the street. His buckboard's over at Mike Carey's store, fully loaded. Mike's outside, enjoying a cigarette. Of the Pinkerton legend, there's no damn sign.'

20

Bywater caught Nathan Wedge as he was mounting his horse outside the bank premises. Contrary to expectations, the banker's face seemed wiped clean of all anxiety. No steel now, but a lot of quiet pleasure. When he saw Bywater, a smile came readily to his face.

'Your efforts and my promises were all rather pointless,' he said, leaning on the saddle horn. 'I didn't get the nomination.'

'*You* didn't?' Bywater couldn't keep the surprise from his voice. 'Neither did Millard Jackson — so I guess the powers who make these decisions picked another man.'

'Goddamn,' Wedge said. 'Now why does that give me an immense feeling of relief?'

It was his parting shot. He pointed his horse down the street, heading,

Bywater assumed, for a big white house on the North Platte. Then, dismissing the banker from his mind, he continued up the street to the saloon.

It was late afternoon. The sun was still high, but the shadows of the town's tall false fronts were already falling across the street. For Temple Bywater, setting out on a task for which he had no enthusiasm, those shadows were creating an aura of gloom. He stepped inside Ike Adams's establishment experiencing a feeling he supposed was not unlike that of a man facing a firing squad. When he caught sight of the huge, flamboyant figure leaning with his elbows on the bar, six-gun jutting from his hip, he knew the comparison could be frighteningly close to the truth.

The place was empty. Texas Jack heard the doors open and close, and twisted his head to look back without altering his posture. What struck Bywater at once was the muted nature of the man's greeting. There was no roar of welcome, no fierce command shouted at Ike Adams to 'set up the drinks for my good friend.' Instead, Texas Jack watched his approach from that same twisted position — and made no comment at all when Bywater walked to the end of the bar, deliberately putting a clear fifteen feet of space between himself and Texas Jack.

'Let me guess,' Texas Jack said, turning to face Bywater. 'You were in my cabin, and you spotted my mistake.'

'I spotted it, but didn't see the significance. Bony's more resourceful. He took a closer look.'

'Bless him,' Texas Jack said. 'I must remember to give him my thanks when I'm finished here.'

'When you're finished here,' Bywater said, 'you're finished for good.'

Texas Jack nodded thoughtfully. He gestured to the watching Ike Adams.

'Give my friend a drink, Ike.' He looked sideways at Bywater. 'For old times' sake?'

'Oh, yes. We've shared the good and the bad, over the years, and I'll gladly drink to all those times. But when that's done, I'm taking you in for the murder of Andrew Stone.'

'Jesus Christ,' Ike Adams whispered.

Texas Jack grimaced. 'What would you have done, Temp, if a man robbed you blind?'

'I would have taken back what was mine, there and then, and walked away.'

'Stone left me for dead,' Texas Jack said, and nodded affirmation as Bywater registered shock. 'He used an iron bar on me. I took six months to recover. When I worked up the strength to climb back on a horse, Stone was long gone.'

'Was finding him here in Saratoga pure accident?'

'Of course. Hell, I didn't even recognize him when I saw him in town. Then I heard his name mentioned . . . '

He shrugged, tossed back his drink and turned to face Bywater.

'Stealing that plaque was foolish, but symbolic. I couldn't get at his money — or even that part of it that was my money — but I needed something that would be a constant reminder that the man had paid for what he did. I hung the damn thing over my bed. I could see it, see his name in the glow of the lamp, and I must admit that after a time I grew to hate it. When you arrived I'd almost got around to convincing myself I should throw it away, dump it in the river. Another day or two — '

'Enough,' Bywater said. He ceremoniously raised his glass to the big man, tossed back the drink, then slammed down the empty glass.

'Unbuckle your gunbelt, Jack, it's time to — '

'No. Sorry, Temp. It doesn't work like that.'

'I know. But I had to try' — Bywater smiled faintly — 'for old times' sake.'

Temple Jack echoed the smile, then stepped away from the bar.

'I'm about to walk out of here, Temp. Straight out the door. What are you going to do to stop me? Shoot me in the back?'

'If that's what it takes.'

'Don't be a bloody fool, Jack,' Ike Adams said hoarsely.

His words fell into a pool of deathly silence. For a moment it seemed as if Texas Jack was seriously considering the saloonist's advice. Then he smiled wryly, and shook his head.

'You know, I really think you'd do it,' he said — and without wasting the time it would take to blink an eye, he went for his six-gun.

He was a big man, Texas Jack Logan. His hands were like slabs of beef. His holster was set too high on his hip. His pistol was as big as a cannon, a massive hunk of cold steel. All of this Bywater knew. But he had seen Texas Jack outdraw lean outlaws from south of the border, had watched him spin on heel and toe to down a New York gangster who had come up on him from behind with a hideaway derringer.

He had never seen him beaten.

So it was with an icy frisson of fear that he watched the big man's hand stab towards his holster. And then, in an extraordinary way, Temple Bywater became detached.

He didn't will his own right hand to move. As if of its own accord it rose from its relaxed position alongside his thigh to brush the butt of his six-gun. The relaxed arm was still bending when his fingers coiled around the Colt's wooden grip. In a silkily smooth continuation of the movement, the six-gun was drawn from its supple leather holster. As it rose, Bywater's thumb curved over the hammer and cocked the action. And, while all this was happening — taking the merest fraction of a second — as if staring into a mirror he could see Texas Jack Morgan going though exactly the same sequence of exquisitely precise movements.

Later, he would try to determine if he had gazed across that fifteen foot gap and seen in Texas Jack's eyes a certain resignation. He would ask himself if he had seen the shadow of a smile flicker across the big man's face — as he deliberately slowed down his draw.

Or was it, Temple Bywater would also ask himself, necessary justification? Was he desperately hanging on to the belief that Texas Jack Logan had deliberately allowed himself to be beaten to the draw to absolve himself of all blame for the killing of a friend, and a Pinkerton legend?

For that, as the fraction of a second that had passed since Texas Jack's first movement ended in shattering climax, was what he did.

Bywater's pistol came level. Still detached, he saw Texas Jack's hunk of lethal metal that was his big .44 Dragoon flick weightlessly out of the awkward, hip-high holster. The huge black hole in the muzzle gaped at him. Texas Jack snapped back the hammer.

Temple Bywater pulled the trigger.

The bullet flew fifteen feet, and slammed into Texas Jack's chest. The big man's chin dropped. His mouth gaped. The heavy pistol drooped in his hand. Then it fell with a thud into the sawdust. Texas Jack staggered sideways. His body slammed into the bar, shaking its length. On the other side, Ike Adams reached out a hand as if to steady the dying man. Then Texas Jack slid down. As if unutterably tired, and in desperate need of a rest, he sat down with his back against the bar. And there, with a long sigh, he died.

His eyes blurred, Temple Bywater sent his six-gun bouncing across the sawdust floor, turned away from his dead friend and walked blindly out into the afternoon sunlight.

THE END

We do hope that you have enjoyed reading this large print book.

Did you know that all of our titles are available for purchase?

We publish a wide range of high quality large print books including:
Romances, Mysteries, Classics
General Fiction
Non Fiction and Westerns

Special interest titles available in large print are:
The Little Oxford Dictionary
Music Book, Song Book
Hymn Book, Service Book

Also available from us courtesy of Oxford University Press:
Young Readers' Dictionary
(large print edition)
Young Readers' Thesaurus
(large print edition)

For further information or a free brochure, please contact us at:
Ulverscroft Large Print Books Ltd.,
The Green, Bradgate Road, Anstey,
Leicester, LE7 7FU, England.
Tel: (00 44) **0116 236 4325**
Fax: (00 44) **0116 234 0205**

Other titles in the
Linford Western Library:

RUNNING CROOKED

Corba Sunman

Despite his innocence, Taw Landry served five years in prison for robbery. Freed at last, his troubles seemed over, but when he reached the home range, they were just beginning. He was determined to discover who'd stolen twenty thousand dollars from the stage office in Cottonwood. But Taw's resolution was overtaken by events. Murder was committed and rustling was rife as Taw tried to unravel the five-year-old mystery. As the guns began to blaze — could he survive to the final showdown?